THE A & A DETECTIVE AGENCY

THE FAIRFLEET AFFAIR

THE A & A DETECTIVE AGENCY

THE FAIRFLEET AFFAIR

K. H. SAXTON

To Phoebe—

Enjoy the mystery!

K. H. Saxton

union
square
kids

NEW YORK

union
square
kids

NEW YORK

ISBN 978-1-4549-5012-7 (hardcover)
ISBN 978-1-4549-5013-4 (paperback)
ISBN 978-1-4549-5014-1 (e-book)

Library of Congress Control Number: 2022054854

For information about custom editions, special sales, and premium
purchases, please contact specialsales@unionsquareandco.com.

Printed in the United States of America

Lot #:
2   4   6   8   10   9   7   5   3   1

07/23

unionsquareandco.com

Cover and interior design by Julie Robine
Additional image credits: iStock/Getty Images Plus: emilio100 (ram),
FARBAI (fish), Kreangagirl (birds) (page 169)

For Neil, my partner in all of life's mysteries

CONTENTS

Prologue   1

Chapter 1: The Archivist   10

Chapter 2: Introduction to Museum Studies   31

Chapter 3: *La Grenouille de l'étang*   53

Chapter 4: Dramatic Action   73

Chapter 5: Wrong Turns and Red Herrings   89

Chapter 6: The Clock Tower   106

Chapter 7: Excessive Heat Warning   121

Chapter 8: A Rare and Valuable Thing   140

Chapter 9: How to Break into the Fairfleet Mansion   159

Chapter 10: The Excavation of Xavier Fairfleet   179

Chapter 11: Of Feathers and Frogs   198

Chapter 12: The Lake House   218

Chapter 13: The Truth, as They Say, Will Out   232

Epilogue   254

PROLOGUE

Saturday, June 10th

On a typical day in the town of Northbrook there were no mysteries to speak of, but on the tenth of June there were three:

In the first place, June 10th marked the start of summer vacation for Northbrook public school students, yet the streets and parks—which should have been filled with laughter and celebratory shrieks, the skittering of sprinklers, the beat of jump ropes on pavement, and the occasional pop and splatter of water balloons—were instead empty and eerily silent. The few children who ventured outdoors looked up and around with grave curiosity before retreating. Even the birds were songless and subdued, hidden away in the summer foliage.

In the second place, on the morning of June 10th a solar eclipse passed over the town. The citizens of Northbrook, stoic New Englanders, were not generally given to superstition. Still, it was hard to shake the feeling that some dark sign or omen could be read in the alignment of sun, moon, and Earth. This second, celestial mystery may well have explained the strange summer silence of the first. Total darkness lasted for only a few minutes; the uncanny dimness and nervous hush that descended upon Northbrook lingered all day.

In the third place, and more to the point, the tenth of June was the day that Dr. Alistair Fairfleet went missing.

The disappearance of Dr. Fairfleet was the biggest scandal to hit Northbrook in decades. He had been scheduled to give a report to the Waverly College board of trustees on the progress and initiatives of the celebrated museums of the Fairfleet Institute. When he failed to show up to his own presentation, the board immediately knew something was amiss. In the nearly thirty years that he had served as chairman of the Institute, Dr. Alistair Fairfleet had never been late to an appointment.

When the police searched his mansion, they found no sign of forced entry. His car—a black sedan, strangely sensible for a millionaire—was still in the garage. A bowl of Frosted Mini-Wheats sat half-eaten on the breakfast bar. Wherever he may have gone, whatever may have happened to him, he left behind his beloved cat with only a day's worth of food and water. As Alistair Fairfleet had never missed an appointment, so Captain Nemo had never missed a meal.

Both the town and the college threw considerable resources at the case. The Fairfleet family was one of the oldest, and unquestionably the richest, in Northbrook. The museums of the Fairfleet Institute were the crown jewels of Waverly College. Unfortunately, the police had little to go on. No canny kidnapper had contacted the authorities with ransom demands. Dr. Fairfleet himself had left behind no note, no clue as to his whereabouts. Or so everyone thought.

Exactly three weeks after Dr. Alistair Fairfleet's disappearance, four identical letters were delivered to four unsuspecting recipients. The morning of July 1st was sunny and mild—not an eclipse in sight. The twittering of birds heralded a day of fine weather and unwelcome surprises.

Dr. Prudence Ito, director of the Fairfleet Museum of Art, read her letter while sitting in her solarium and drinking her morning coffee, black. She frowned as she scanned the note, drumming her fingers on the ceramic tiles that covered the table. The tiles, imported from Turkey, were exquisite replicas of sixteenth-century Iznik pottery pieces. Dr. Prudence Ito tapped her fingers so hard that she chipped one of her neatly manicured nails without registering that she had done so. She had more important things to worry about.

Minnie Mayflower, principal archivist of the Fairfleet Historical Archives, perused her letter from the comfort of her favorite armchair. She sipped her English breakfast tea with one spoon of sugar and a dash of milk. Her hands shook a little as she stroked the black-and-white cat curled up in her lap. When she finished reading, she set the letter on the coffee table and wrapped herself more tightly in her cardigan. Although the day promised to be warm and Minnie was a young woman in good health, she felt cold. The cat, disturbed by her movements, gave a disdainful *mrowl* and leapt down from her lap to find a more agreeable place to nap.

Quentin Carlisle, artistic director of the Fairfleet Center for the Performing Arts, slept late on the morning of the first. The FCPA's production of *Arsenic and Old Lace* had closed the previous evening, and the strain of answering the press's questions about Alistair Fairfleet combined with the excitement of closing night had left him worn-out.

Squinting against the late-morning light, he poured himself a glass of orange juice and added just a splash of something stronger from a silver flask. As he read his letter, what little color was left in his cheeks drained entirely. He thought for a moment, then poured several more glugs from the flask into his juice.

Dr. John Wright, executive curator of the Fairfleet Museum of Natural History, had not slept at all. He had spent the night in his office with only the looming dinosaur fossils outside his door for company. Dr. Wright was a man of many firsts: the first Oxford-educated anthropologist at Waverly College, the first Black director of a Fairfleet museum, and the first non-Fairfleet to run the Museum of Natural History specifically. He was also the first to assume many of Dr. Fairfleet's responsibilities in the chairman's absence—hence his sleepless night in the museum.

When Dr. Wright finally noticed the letter on the corner of his desk, he could not say how or when it had arrived. He took a sip from the thermos that his wife, Martha, had made up for him the night before. Its contents, once hot and home-brewed, were now tepid and tasteless. Dr. Wright slit the creamy envelope with a nineteenth-century letter opener. Upon reading the message, he let out a derisive snort. He crumpled the letter into a ball and threw it at the trash can in the corner, missing by a wide margin. For two full minutes he glowered and grumbled in his chair; then he retrieved the crumpled ball of paper and smoothed it out on his desk. He read the message over several more times while the dinosaurs kept their watch.

By noon on July 1st all four recipients had read their four identical letters. All four recipients now had more information about Alistair Fairfleet's disappearance than the entire Northbrook police force had gathered in three weeks, and none of them had any intention of sharing what they had learned. This is what the letter said:

Dear Sir or Madam,

If you are receiving this letter, it is because I, Dr. Alistair Fairfleet, chairman of the Fairfleet Institute, have disappeared under suspicious circumstances. You are the director of one of the official branches of the Fairfleet Institute. Your counterparts have received this letter as well. You have served the Institute admirably in your role. Now I require assistance of a different sort. I am afraid that I am in no position to communicate with you directly. Nevertheless, I have critical information to share with you all. The truth, as they say, will out.

Two of you share a secret that has been kept in the shadows for too long. One of you will succeed me as chair of the Fairfleet Institute. And one of you, alas, is responsible for my sudden disappearance. To find out who is who and which is which, you will have to follow the trail I've left. Your first clue is enclosed in your envelope.

Perhaps you are not inclined to participate in the hunt. Perhaps you feel that it would be safer or easier or wiser to leave the earth undisturbed and let these secrets remain buried. I am not unsympathetic to your view. Like it or not, however, we are all players in this game and have been for quite some time. Participation is not optional.

It is imperative that you find the solution and come to my aid on July 15th. By design, you cannot arrive early, but I beg you, for my sake, not to be late. Do not contact the police.

Their involvement would be neither in your best interest nor in mine.

Thank you for your time and attention. I advise you to consider your enclosed clue with due urgency.

Regards,

Dr. Alistair Fairfleet

With this letter safely in the hands of its intended readers, a fifth almost-but-not-quite-identical message was delivered. Alex Foster and Asha Singh of the A&A Detective Agency received it at noon on the dot. While most of the letter had been copied word for word from the original, there were three notable differences.

In the first place, Dr. Fairfleet had slipped a small prefix into the first paragraph to reflect the A&A Detective Agency's status as an *un*official branch of the Fairfleet Institute. Alistair Fairfleet was the detectives' primary investor, but this pet project was neither known to nor recognized by the Waverly College board.

In the second place, the letter was not hand-delivered but was instead sent to the agency's email address. Alex and Asha took the professionalism of their agency very seriously, but they were also twelve years old. They were obliged, for the time being, to operate out of Alex's tree house.

In the third place, Alistair Fairfleet had been unable to resist showing a bit of favoritism in the closing of his otherwise formal message:

```
Thank you for your time and attention. I
advise you to consider your enclosed clue with
due urgency.

Good luck!
Dr. Alistair Fairfleet
```

CHAPTER 1

THE ARCHIVIST

Saturday, July 1st

As an office space for a detective agency, Alex Foster's tree house was not, perhaps, perfectly practical. As a tree house, however, it was practically perfect. It was built in a giant oak in the Fosters' backyard, a grandfatherly tree with a thick trunk and sprawling branches made for climbing. The tree house had everything a tree house ought to have: a rope ladder and a trapdoor, wide floor planks that smelled of cedar, a periscope that peeked out through the leaves for spying on passersby—as well as a number of unique amenities: a wall lined with bookshelves, a cozy hammock strung up in the corner, and a single solar panel that powered a heat lamp in the winter and a fan in the summer.

Alex was fiercely protective of the tree house. He had a strict "no strangers allowed" policy that he had broken only once in a calculated effort to befriend the unflappable new girl with the long black braid.

Asha, for her part, had known she liked the tree house before she knew she liked Alex. When she had moved to the neighborhood back in third grade, it was one of the first things that made her feel at home. She liked Alex's family too. His mother was a history professor at Waverly College, and his father ran the local newspaper, *The Northbrook Nail*. He had a baby brother named Ollie and an old, blind border collie named Don Quixote— Donkey for short. Asha envied the warmth and bustle of the Foster household. Things were pretty quiet at her house. She was an only child, and her father was allergic to most pets.

When Alex first met Asha, he found her easy to talk to and hard to impress—perfect best-friend material. When Asha first met Alex, she wished he were a little *harder* to impress so that maybe he would stop talking to her so much, but she decided that no one with such a wonderful tree house could be that bad. And she had been right. Alex had a knack for adventure and a borderline dangerous imagination. As it turned out, being friends with Alex Foster was well worth the occasional exasperation.

After lunch on the afternoon of July 1st, the agents of the A&A Detective Agency sat across from each other in the tree house on oversized beanbag chairs. They had printed the mysterious email from Dr. Fairfleet, and it now lay on the floor between them. It had been sent not from Dr. Fairfleet's email address but from one of those pesky "no reply" addresses with the domain @ALB.org. The URL led nowhere, and ALB didn't ring any bells. Asha had a little notebook and a pencil for jotting down notes and ideas. Alex didn't believe in taking notes, and if he did, he would never choose to write them on paper like some sort of troglodyte.

"Should we tell our parents?" Alex asked reluctantly.

Asha frowned. "I don't think so. Telling our parents is as good as telling the police, and Dr. Fairfleet specifically said we shouldn't talk to the police."

"Right. That's what I thought." Alex scratched his elbow and fidgeted in his beanbag chair. "But if he's in trouble, don't you think we should let an adult know?"

"Since when do you trust adults?"

"Since when do you not?"

It was a fair question. Alex's family had known Dr. Fairfleet for years. Asha's mother was a well-connected attorney in Northbrook. Showing any of their parents the letter would have been the responsible option. The easy option.

"Look," Asha conceded with a shrug, "I know this is a bit beyond our pay grade." That was the understatement of the year, and they both knew it. They didn't *have* a pay grade. The only person ever to pay them for their detective work was Dr. Fairfleet, who once gave them ten dollars apiece for finding an heirloom watch that he had hidden just so Asha and Alex might have a case to solve. "At least we have a list of adults that we can consult."

"What we have," Alex argued, "is a list of suspects."

Attached to the email from Dr. Fairfleet was a file: "EnclosedClue.pdf." Asha had copied the information into her notebook with meticulous care. Their clue was a list of four names:

Quentin Carlisle
Prudence Ito
Minnie Mayflower
John Wright

"It's a starting place. We also have a deadline: July 15th. That gives us exactly two weeks to figure everything out." Asha didn't know what Dr. Fairfleet meant when he said that *by design* they couldn't arrive early, but she understood the chilling implications of *"I beg you, for my sake, not to be late."*

"Are we taking the case?" A small light flickered in Alex's eyes, the sort of light that is kindled when someone with a general suspicion of rules finds a compelling reason to break one.

"I think we have to." Asha, unlike Alex, had a healthy respect for rules, but she had a healthier respect for Dr. Fairfleet. The chairman had welcomed the children of Northbrook to his museums for decades. He was one of those rare adults who never made Alex and Asha feel underestimated or overlooked. Now he was asking for their help in the form of a secret email—a cry for help, a call to action. They wouldn't let him down.

Alex stood up and stretched, reaching for the ceiling. He was small for his age and took every opportunity to maximize his height. Asha suspected that was why he kept his sandy curls on the long side: for the extra inch. "Where do you want to start?" he asked. "With the most suspicious or the least suspicious?"

Asha folded her arms without budging from her bean-bag chair. "I don't think we have enough information to make those sorts of judgments yet."

"C'mon. I mean, we know it's not Minnie."

"Do we?" Asha asked, more to irritate Alex than anything else. Minnie Mayflower had been Alex's baby-sitter for years, starting when she was an undergraduate at Waverly College. Minnie was pretty and sweet, and Alex was loyal to those he admired. Asha knew that over-coming Alex's bias where Minnie was concerned was going to be one of their first obstacles. "Sometimes it's the suspects who seem most innocent who have the most to hide."

"In books and movies, maybe. Not in real life. Not Minnie."

Asha's gaze flickered toward the ceiling, but she stopped just short of rolling her eyes. "That's fine. Starting with Minnie is probably our best bet anyway. Since she knows us, she's more likely to talk to us. We're going to have to work our way up to Dr. Ito and Dr. Wright."

"Work up the courage, you mean." Alex smirked. "Because you're scared of them."

"I am *not* scared of them."

"You are. A little," Alex needled, searching for a weak point in Asha's armor. He didn't press too hard. Truth be told, he was intimidated by Dr. Ito and Dr. Wright himself.

Ignoring the hand that Alex offered, Asha crossed her legs, shifted her weight, and stood up in one smooth motion. She climbed down the rope ladder without looking back up at him, her braid swinging behind her like the tail of a cat.

Because it was Saturday, Alex and Asha didn't know if Minnie would be at home or at work. Fortunately, it didn't much matter. Minnie lived in a small apartment above the Waverly College Library, where the Fairfleet Historical Archives were housed. They rode their bicycles to the library in the hot afternoon sun. The door to the archives was locked, so Asha and Alex went up a back staircase to knock on the door of Minnie's apartment. The door swung open to reveal a surprised archivist.

"Alex? Goodness! What are you doing here?" Minnie's blue eyes were wide behind gold-framed glasses. Her strawberry blond hair was tied back in a sleek knot, and she wore a lilac cardigan over a sundress with a dragonfly print.

"Hi, Minnie. You remember Asha Singh? Do you mind if we come in?"

Minnie took note of Alex's red, sweaty face and the glaring sun. "Yes, of course. Come in where it's cool, and I'll get you some lemonade. Do your parents know you're here?"

"They don't expect me home until dinner," Alex replied evasively.

Alex and Asha made themselves at home on Minnie's couch. Or rather, Alex made himself at home. Asha sat on the edge of the cushion, back straight, aware that they had not really been invited over.

Minnie's apartment looked like what might happen if someone's grandmother's house were made over by woodland fairies. Crocheted pillows and quilts covered most available seating. Vases and mason jars filled with wildflowers adorned the coffee table and any free spaces on the crowded bookshelf. The apartment smelled faintly of lavender and strongly of old paper.

Minnie returned from the kitchen carrying a tray with two glasses of lemonade and a ham sandwich cut into quarters. Ham and Swiss with mustard was Alex's favorite, as Minnie must have remembered. Asha didn't eat meat, but she gratefully accepted the lemonade, which was oversweet but still cold and refreshing.

"Now then," Minnie said, sitting down in the velvet armchair across from them. "What brings you two to my door on this sunny summer day?"

Asha sipped her lemonade while Alex took the lead. "We know about Dr. Fairfleet's letter."

Minnie turned pale, and her wide eyes grew even wider. To her credit, however, she did not try to deny anything. Instead she replied, "How on earth could you know about that?"

Asha held out the printed email for Minnie to inspect. "Because we got one too."

"We're with the A&A Detective Agency. Maybe you've heard of us?" Alex asked.

"Oh." Minnie blinked as she glanced from the letter to the expectant look on Alex's face. "I'm quite sure I have, but why don't you . . . remind me."

"We started the agency last year during the Fairfleet Summer Program," Asha said. "We got the idea when Dr. Fairfleet said that Northbrook didn't have a private detective agency. He's our principal investor, you know. He gave us lots of books to read—Agatha Christie, Sir Arthur Conan Doyle, that sort of thing. And he bought us some business cards and printed an ad for us in *The Northbrook Nail.*"

Alex shuffled around in his pocket and pulled out a crumpled business card, which he handed to Minnie. The business card featured their contact information and a graphic of a private eye in a trench coat and fedora that Alex had designed himself.

Minnie took a moment to read the card before graciously placing it in her purse. "That's very enterprising of you. What drew you to detective work, if I may ask?"

There were many answers to this question. Asha could have said that she aspired to be in the FBI one day. She wanted to be tough and honest and prove her male colleagues wrong. Alex could have said that he believed robots would one day render most jobs obsolete and that consulting detective work seemed as good a way as any to pass the time in a fully automated future.

Asha offered a simpler explanation. "We needed something to do. School is pretty easy."

"And pretty boring," Alex added. Whereas most teachers found Asha's bookishness endearing, Alex's rebellious intelligence tended to make adults nervous. There was only so much amusement to be had in provoking frazzled Mrs. Doncaster.

"Dr. Fairfleet thought that detective work might provide a nice challenge for us," Asha continued. "But to be honest, we haven't had many cases yet. Nothing real."

"Until now," Alex said.

"Until now," Minnie echoed. "I see."

"So, will you let us help?" Asha asked.

Minnie took off her glasses and held the heel of her hand to her forehead as though warding off a headache. Alex hoped she wouldn't cry. He wasn't sure he could handle a tearful Minnie.

"I really don't know what to say." Minnie put her glasses back on and tucked a stray strand of copper hair behind her ear. "I think it's admirable that you want to help Dr. Fairfleet, but we don't know what sort of trouble he might be in. I've considered going to the police despite his warning. It's just . . ." She paused. "Well, I remembered that Dr. Fairfleet squabbled with the chief of police last summer over the Fourth of July concert on the Green."

Alex sat bolt upright. "You think the police could be in on it? Like a conspiracy?" Alex adored a good conspiracy.

"I don't know. It sounds so silly when you say it out loud," Minnie replied, wringing the hem of her cardigan.

At that moment, a black-and-white ball of fur hopped up on Asha's lap. The furball stretched and settled into the form of a snoozing cat. Cats had always liked Asha, and Asha had always liked cats. Alex was more of a dog person—or maybe a lizard person.

"Who's this?" Asha cooed, stroking the cat's silky head.

"That's Captain Nemo, Dr. Fairfleet's cat," Minnie said. "I often cat-sit for Dr. Fairfleet, so after he went missing, I decided to bring Captain Nemo back here. I'm afraid he's quite out of sorts. Every time I open the door, he tries to run home. I've had to retrieve him from Dr. Fairfleet's mansion three times this week."

Asha made a mental note: *Minnie has a key to Dr. Fairfleet's house.*

Alex made a mental note: *Everybody likes cats except for me.*

"Minnie," Alex began, "Dr. Fairfleet must've sent the letter to us for a reason, but we won't know what that reason is if you don't let us help."

"Maybe you could show us your clue?" Asha suggested. "Just a peek?"

Minnie hesitated. "I suppose there's no harm in that. Dr. Fairfleet has always worked in mysterious ways."

She stood up and left the living room, returning a minute later with her letter. Unlike Alex and Asha's email, Minnie's letter was printed on heavy, cream-colored stationery stamped with Alistair Fairfleet's personal seal. Minnie placed a second piece of the same stationery on the coffee table. Asha and Alex both leaned forward to get a better look, and a disgruntled Captain Nemo dislodged himself from Asha's lap. On the piece of creamy paper there was a short quotation written in deep blue ink:

> *"Unhappy that I am, I cannot heave*
> *my heart into my mouth."* W. S.

At the bottom of the page there was a postscript:

> **Gather all the pieces and put them*
> *in order, but don't ignore your*
> *initial observations.*

Asha read over the clue, mouthing the words. She wasn't sure what it meant, but it had a nice ring to it. "W. S.," she said. "Minnie, is this William Shakespeare?"

"It is indeed."

"Shakespeare?" Alex groaned. After watching a particularly dull community theater production of *The Tempest*, Alex had a poor opinion of the Bard.

Minnie gave him a pursed-lip smile. "Shakespeare's not so bad. This quotation is from *King Lear*, one of my favorite plays."

"Why is your clue a Shakespeare quotation?" Asha asked .

"Maybe she's supposed to look inside a copy of the play," Alex suggested.

"If that's the case, I don't know what copy Dr. Fairfleet had in mind. Both of mine seem to be dead ends." Minnie gestured toward two books on the coffee table: a large hardcover edition of *The Riverside Shakespeare* and a paperback copy of *King Lear*. Alex picked up the smaller of the two and flipped through the worn pages. The margins were packed with penciled-in notes and questions.

"The annotations are my own," Minnie assured him. "I spent all morning combing through them to be sure. And there's nothing at all in the *Riverside*."

"The note at the bottom says to 'gather all the pieces.' I guess you've got to get more pieces somehow—more clues. We should find out what Dr. Fairfleet left for the other directors."

Asha had been silently rehearsing the line, committing it to memory. "What does it *mean*, though?" she asked.

"The quotation?" Minnie folded her hands in her lap. "Well, in the play, King Lear is the aging king of Britain who is trying to decide how to divide his kingdom. His ego gets the best of him, and he hands over his land and power to his two cruel daughters, who flatter him, instead of his honest daughter, who loves him. In this quotation, the good daughter, Cordelia, is explaining that she is unable to use empty words to express what she feels in her heart."

"If that's what Shakespeare meant, why didn't he just say it like a normal person?" Alex complained.

"In a way," Asha mused, "Dr. Fairfleet is sort of like the aging king of the Fairfleet Institute."

Alex saw where her train of thought was headed and jumped aboard. "Sure! And he said in his letter that one of the recipients would take over as head of the Institute. Was Dr. Fairfleet thinking of retiring?"

"I wouldn't know," Minnie admitted as she absently traced the seal on her letter. "Professionally speaking, I wouldn't have access to that information. I'm not exactly next in line for the throne. And personally . . . what I mean to say is . . . Dr. Fairfleet and I don't have the sort of relationship where he might confide such things to me. We don't have much of a personal relationship at all."

"You take care of his cat," Asha reminded her.

Alex did not see how the cat was relevant. "Who *would* be most likely to take over after Dr. Fairfleet? Or who would want to the most?"

"I suppose the answer to both of those questions would be John Wright. He's extremely qualified, and he's never been shy about his ambitions within the Institute. Of course, Prudence Ito has also done tremendous work for the art museum. She's very popular with the Waverly College board."

"The letter almost makes it sound like a competition. What if whoever solves the mystery and saves Dr. Fairfleet gets to be his successor?"

"I'm afraid it couldn't possibly be that simple," Minnie said, crushing Asha's spun-glass theory. "The logistics of Dr. Fairfleet's retirement are . . . thorny, to say the least."

"What do you mean, 'thorny'?"

"It's all to do with the Fairfleet Charter. Complicated legal business. I wouldn't want to bore you with it. Are you two still hungry? Would you like some Oreos?"

"No thank you," Asha said, at the same moment that Alex said, "Yes, please!"

Smoothing the skirt of her sundress, Minnie stood up and took the empty plate to the kitchen.

"She seems nervous," Asha observed.

"She seems *anxious*," Alex replied. "You know, because her boss disappeared and left her a mysterious letter that implies she has something to hide."

"Maybe she does have something to hide."

Minnie's return cut short their conversation. Asha accepted an Oreo—mostly to be polite—and nibbled at it unenthusiastically. Alex began twisting his cookies apart, eating the chocolate rounds and saving the stack of cream centers for later.

"Would you please tell us about the Fairfleet Charter?" Asha asked.

"It won't bore us," Alex assured her.

"If you insist," Minnie said, taking an Oreo for herself. "As you may know, the first branch of the Fairfleet Institute was the Museum of Natural History, which was founded by Wadsworth Fairfleet in 1830. The Fairfleets had been prosperous farmers since the colonial period, but it was Wadsworth's textile mill that made them one of the wealthiest families in America. The museum was his true legacy, however. When Wadsworth wrote and signed the charter, he set up the terms of inheritance so that only a Fairfleet could take over as chair of the Institute."

"That sounds downright feudal," Alex noted. "Not very American, anyway."

"Wadsworth Fairfleet was both a dreamer and a realist," Minnie said with a weak smile, "not unlike another Fairfleet we all know. I believe he wanted to keep much of the family fortune tied up in the museum. Furthermore, he wanted to ensure that his children and grandchildren would have a sense of purpose and responsibility even though they were born into great privilege."

"But our Dr. Fairfleet isn't married. He doesn't have any children," Asha said.

"Hence the thorny problem of his retirement. It's never been an issue until now because there's always been a Fairfleet waiting in the wings. Of course, there was the matter of Dr. Fairfleet's great-grandmother, I believe." Minnie quickly tallied the generations on her fingers. "Maude Fairfleet caused quite a scandal in Northbrook by taking over after her husband's death when their son was still a baby, but she was also a visionary chairwoman. She founded the Fairfleet Museum of Art in 1902, and—"

"Minnie," Alex cut her off, sensing that the archivist had taken a side path that she could follow endlessly through the twisted groves of Northbrook's history. "What does all of this mean for Dr. Fairfleet?"

"It means that we're in uncharted—or unchartered—territory." Minnie adjusted her glasses. "The charter is a document like any other. It can be revised or taken to court if necessary. However, Wadsworth Fairfleet was very thorough when he laid out his stipulations. There's complicated language about what should happen in the absence of a Fairfleet heir."

"Like what?" Asha asked.

"Goodness. I'm sure I don't remember. The charter is kept in the archives, though. We could go take a look at it if you want." Minnie's expression was cautiously hopeful, as if she couldn't quite believe that two twelve-year-old children would be interested in her archival passion.

"Of course we want to!" Alex stood up too quickly, scattering cookie crumbs all over the floor.

"How exciting!" Minnie flushed and clasped her hands together. "I can't believe I didn't think to look sooner. Follow me, please!"

Minnie led the pair of amateur sleuths through her small apartment and down a private staircase to the archives. Alex and Asha had been to the archives once before on a school tour. There was a long central hallway, narrow and dimly lit. To Asha, the archives were mysterious and inviting, as though the boxes would whisper secrets to someone with better hearing. To Alex, the archives were unsettling, as though he had stumbled into the basement of a well-organized hoarder—which, in a sense, he had.

"Welcome to the Wadsworth Stacks," Minnie said. "Named after the great Wadsworth Fairfleet himself."

Branching off from the corridor were the stacks in question—enormous shelves that could be moved with large hand cranks to allow for more compact storage. The shelves were lined with archival boxes, and the air was cool and dry. In the central aisle, the trio had to navigate around several glass cases containing old documents and photographs related to the history of Northbrook and the Fairfleet family. The displays were a bit dusty and poorly lit.

Alex examined some of the items on display: Hand-drawn maps of Northbrook from when it was just a colonial village. A list of Northbrook men and boys who had fought in the Civil War. He stopped in front of a graying sheet of numerical code from World War II. Alex's interest in computer coding was rooted in a much deeper love of codes and code-breaking; he could spend hours talking about the history of military ciphers.

Asha was more interested in a different set of numbers. She had noticed that the stacks were labeled with dates—a different decade for every set of shelves.

Minnie caught her examining the placards and explained, "Our catalog system was created specifically for the Wadsworth Stacks. Items are organized into files, and every file is assigned a number that begins with the date of acquisition.

Even the charter has a number. Of course, we don't keep the charter in a file anymore."

They had reached the end of the long hallway. Ahead of them, framed by a halo of low light, was an oil painting of a man with a top hat and impressive sideburns.

"And here's Wadsworth Fairfleet!" With a knowing wink, Minnie swung the portrait away from the wall to reveal an old-fashioned safe. "If I could have a moment of privacy."

The detectives turned their backs while Minnie worked the combination lock. When Alex attempted a furtive look over his shoulder, he received a sharp elbow in the ribs from Asha.

After a moment, the lock gave way with a metallic click, and the safe door creaked open.

"Oh," Minnie said. "Oh dear."

Asha and Alex spun around. Minnie's shoulders sagged. Disappointment and panic were battling it out on her face, but panic seemed to be winning.

The safe was empty.

The Fairfleet Charter was gone.

CHAPTER 2

INTRODUCTION TO MUSEUM STUDIES

Sunday, July 2nd

The Fairfleet museums didn't open until noon on Sundays. With several hours to kill before they could talk to Dr. Wright, Alex and Asha met in the tree house to go over the facts as they knew them. Asha made a list in her notebook:

1. The Fairfleet Charter is missing.

2. Dr. Wright wants Dr. Fairfleet's job.

3. Dr. Wright and Dr. Ito are top contenders for Dr. Fairfleet's job.

4. Minnie's first clue is a quote from King Lear.

5. Just because Minnie seems trustworthy doesn't mean that she is.

6. But it also doesn't mean that she's not.

Noon was heralded by the distant tolling of the Trinity Clock on campus. Alex shouted goodbye to his parents while baby Ollie wailed in protest from the other room. Asha grabbed a granola bar from the pantry, and they hopped on their bikes to seek out Dr. Wright.

The Fairfleet Museum of Natural History was, in the humble opinion of both Asha and Alex, the most marvelous place in Northbrook, and quite possibly in the whole world. The museum had four major wings. The Hall of Fossils housed all things prehistoric, most notably the skeletons of several enormous dinosaurs and one mammoth lovingly nicknamed Millicent. The Hall of Planetary Sciences contained the Fairfleet Institute's collection of gemstones as well as some pieces of meteorites, which Alex coveted more than any old diamond. The Hall of Human Origins led visitors on a well-planned walk through the evolution of humanity. But as far as Asha was concerned, none of the other wings could hold a candle to the Hall of Cultural Artifacts. The oldest wing of the museum, the Hall of Cultural Artifacts housed a collection of objects and relics from around the world. Many of the artifacts were gifts, but many more had been collected by generations of Fairfleets as they traversed the globe. Only in the Hall of Cultural Artifacts could one find a Stone Age hand axe, a crumbling Celtic high cross, and a mummified Egyptian cat in adjacent displays.

It seemed a shame to Alex and Asha that the most magical museum in the world was run by someone so utterly lacking in magic himself. Dr. Wright was about as adult as it was possible for an adult to be. He rarely smiled. His voice was deep and serious, and he used words that even Asha had to pretend to understand and then look up later.

They found him in his office, a comfortable, wood-paneled room just past the Hall of Fossils. Hesitating a moment in the shadow of a bony triceratops, Alex worked up the courage to knock on the door.

The door opened without a sound, and the sleuths found themselves looking up at a cross-armed Dr. Wright.

"Mr. Foster. Miss Singh. How may I help you?"

Alex's eyes narrowed. "You know who we are?"

"I've known your parents since before you were born, Mr. Foster," Dr. Wright said. "Minnie Mayflower was kind enough to send all of the other directors a note about your recent meeting. I've been expecting you."

Alex took this news like a stab of betrayal. "Minnie ratted us out?"

"Nonsense! She wanted to make sure there were no more unexpected surprises. We directors are under a great deal of strain. Ms. Mayflower is a bright, thoughtful young woman. Underqualified for her position, but I'm beginning to understand why Alistair hired her."

Asha craned her neck to look past Dr. Wright's stout frame into the warmly lit office behind him. "So . . . can we come in?"

Dr. Wright opened his mouth to protest, but Alex had already ducked under the director's arm and was settling into one of the leather chairs in front of his desk. Asha shrugged as though to say, *kids these days*, and slipped past Dr. Wright to take her seat next to Alex. Dr. Wright sat back down behind his desk. He looked at them over the tops of his steepled fingertips. *Like an angry school principal*, thought Asha. *Like the villain in a Bond film*, thought Alex.

"Let's get right to it, then," Alex said. He produced another business card, which he slapped down on the desktop. "We're from the A&A Detective Agency. We've got some questions for you."

Dr. Wright did not pick up the card, nor did he look impressed. "That won't be necessary, Mr. Foster. I am not interested in Alistair's little game."

Asha scooted her chair closer to the desk. "Game?"

"Alistair can fool the police, and he can fool Minnie Mayflower, but he can't fool me. This whole business reeks of one of his poorly conceived schemes. He's probably off somewhere sipping port, reading novels, and laughing at those of us fussing and fretting over his absence. The fact that he's roped in a couple of junior deputies proves my hypothesis."

Alex appreciated neither the diction nor the tone of the phrase "junior deputies." He glared at the director. "Obviously we thought of that," he said. They obviously hadn't, but it seemed like the sort of thing they *should* have thought of.

Asha jumped in to keep the interrogation rolling. "Even if we decide that Dr. Fairfleet is a suspect in his own disappearance, we still need evidence. And a motive. Right now, the person with the clearest motive is *you*."

Dr. Wright inhaled deeply so that his chest puffed up like a roasting marshmallow. "Why is that? Because I hope to be chairman of the Institute someday? Because I love this museum and everything it stands for? I've been patiently putting in my time for thirty years. Why would I choose now, of all times, to become a common criminal?"

"You could be an extraordinary criminal," Alex said. "No one said anything about being common."

"Did Minnie also tell you that the Fairfleet Charter is missing?" Asha asked.

"She did. And good riddance, I say. That document is a more preposterous relic than anything in this museum. But that doesn't mean I took it," Dr. Wright warned. "Or that I had anything to do with Alistair's disappearance. I assure you that if I knew anything about Alistair's whereabouts, I would have informed the police."

"I suppose you told them about your clue from Dr. Fairfleet, then?" Asha did her best impression of a stern schoolteacher. To her amazement, her strategy worked. Dr. Wright shifted with embarrassment and glanced down at his hands.

"You know very well that I have not," he grumbled.

"If you let us see your clue, maybe we can help you figure it out."

"I've already *figured it out*," Dr. Wright replied with a walrus frown. "However, I'm unwilling to dance to Alistair's tune."

Alex and Asha were both struck speechless. It was astonishing that Dr. Wright had already solved his clue. It was *astounding* that he hadn't yet followed it.

"Oh, close your mouths. You're not at the dentist. Here, take a look if it means that much to you." Dr. Wright opened the top drawer of his desk and took out a small strip of paper. He set the clue on the desk so that Asha and Alex could read it.

We look to the past to know the present.
Examine the first to seek the second.

Asha felt a simmering excitement. "It's a treasure hunt!" she exclaimed. "*Examine the first to seek the second.* There are going to be more clues!"

Alex picked up the strip of paper, flipped it over to inspect the back, and held it up to the light, squinting intently.

"What exactly are you doing?" Dr. Wright asked.

"Examining the first clue for hints about the second one. You always have to check the back of things. That's one of the first rules of detective work."

"Ah, I believe you're barking up the wrong tree." Dr. Wright picked a speck of lint off his tweed jacket. "I've known Alistair since I was a boy. Did you know I grew up in Northbrook?"

There was no reason for Alex and Asha to have known that, and Alex said as much.

"When I was about your age," Dr. Wright continued, "Alistair was the curator of the Museum of Natural History. He used to host scavenger hunts for the young people of Northbrook. He would give clues about different displays and exhibits as a way of drumming up interest in the museum and its collections. It was one of Alistair's more brilliant ideas."

"So the clue is pointing us toward a specific exhibit or artifact?" Asha took the strip of paper from Alex's grasp to get a better look.

"Not just any artifact—the *first* artifact in the Fairfleet collection," said Dr. Wright.

"Wait, I *know* what the oldest piece in the collection is!" Alex's voice was much too loud for the dignified little office. "Dr. Fairfleet told us last summer. It's that old dodo skull, isn't it?" He shut one eye as he tried to remember the details of the lecture. "No, that's not right. Maybe it's the Polynesian fish hook?"

"Or the canopic jar?" Asha suggested.

"No, I've got it!" Alex leapt to his feet in triumph. "It's the carved walrus tusk!"

Dr. Wright confirmed his answer with a gruff nod. "Well done, Mr. Foster. The scrimshaw tusk was carved by a sailor on a New England whaling vessel in the 1700s.

Wadsworth Fairfleet purchased the tusk at auction in 1830 and was inspired to start a small public collection of artifacts—and so the Fairfleet Institute was born."

"Well, what are we waiting for?" cried Alex. "Lead the way, Dr. Wright!"

The director did not budge. "As I mentioned, I do not intend to participate. I am no longer the child Alistair sought to amuse all those years ago."

Asha could feel Alex's anticipation. Her partner was a stone ready to be launched from a slingshot. She looked up slyly at Dr. Wright. "*We're* still children," she observed.

Before the director could respond, Alex and Asha were out of their seats, scampering for the door. Asha noticed that Dr. Wright made no attempt to stop them. She thought that he might have even smiled . . . a little.

The scrimshaw tusk was on a circular plinth near the entrance to the Hall of Cultural Artifacts. The ivory tooth was as long as a human forearm and curved slightly—not as much as an elephant tusk but more than a regular bone. The tusk was engraved with an elaborate sailing ship on one side and a wide whale tail on the other.

"There, look!" Asha pointed at the tip of the tusk, where a small scroll of paper had been rolled around the narrowest end.

They both hesitated. Years of conditioning told them that old, valuable items in museums were not to be touched. The pool of light that surrounded the tusk might as well have been a laser force field. It was Alex who summoned the nerve to breach the boundary. He reached out, slowly at first, then snatched the strip of paper as though the tusk had singed his fingertips.

Asha wouldn't let Alex look at the next clue until they were back in Dr. Wright's office.

"May we read your next clue, please?" Asha asked the director, drawing on her very best manners.

Dr. Wright made them wait as he finished signing a form, took a sip of water, and blew his nose. "If I say no, will it make any difference?"

"Not a chance!" Alex unfurled the little strip of paper and pinned it to the desktop with the tips of both pointer fingers. He read the second clue out loud:

*"That which you seek the terrible ones hold,
the oldest of young and the youngest of old."*

"Don't tell us what it means!" Asha held out an authoritarian hand before the director could speak, though he had made no attempt to do so. "Let us try to figure it out first."

Dr. Wright shrugged. "As you wish."

"The terrible ones hold it," Alex said, half to himself and half to Asha and not at all to Dr. Wright. "What's terrible in this museum?"

"Nothing," Asha replied defensively.

"Perhaps you ought to think about word origins," Dr. Wright proposed.

"We said no hints!" Alex felt his ears go hot. He had the answer now, of course, but his victory would be a hollow one.

"Well?" Dr. Wright leaned back in his chair.

"Dinosaurs," Alex said. "From the Greek *deinos sauros*—terrible lizards. We need to look in the Hall of Fossils."

"Ah, but the Hall of Fossils is our largest wing. Where will you look?"

Asha toyed with the ends of her hair, as she often did when she was thinking. *"The oldest of young and the youngest of old.* Does the museum have any baby dinosaur fossils? Any dinosaur *young*?"

"There's that nest of velociraptor eggs." Alex's eyes gleamed with a rekindled thrill of the hunt. Asha was already tugging at the back of his shirt. They dashed off to test their theory before Dr. Wright could get in another word.

The Hall of Fossils was an echoing cavern of a room. An apatosaurus leered at them from high above, its ribs casting long shadows on the floor. The velociraptor nest was tucked away in one corner, where it was protected by a low glass barrier. Asha spotted the slip of paper nestled in the crevice of a fossilized egg.

They waited impatiently while a museum guard made his rounds and then wandered off to another room. "Give me your hand," Alex prompted. Using Asha for balance, he leaned over the glass enclosure and plucked the clue from the egg. It was easier to cross the imaginary force field the second time around. With their next clue safely in hand, they returned to Dr. Wright's office.

Three hours later, Asha and Alex had discovered six more clues and six more secrets in the Museum of Natural History. Asha was amazed to find one clue attached to the back of a real ruby necklace from Romanov Russia. Alex was more interested in the clue they found in the mouth of a stuffed iguana. Despite his best efforts to remain detached, Dr. Wright had become increasingly invested in the treasure hunt. For the past hour or so, he had been following the detectives from clue to clue, though he never repeated his mistake of offering unwelcome hints.

At 4:00 p.m., just as the museum was scheduled to close, Asha and Alex came across a clue that stumped them, and stumped them hard.

History repeats itself—a saying oft quoted.
While the cat's in the sandbox, the mouse gets promoted.

After she read the couplet, Asha snuck a glance at the executive curator, whose expression had turned grave. "No offense, Dr. Wright, but this clue doesn't look good for you." Asha watched as the director's frown deepened, etching lines in his forehead. "Do you know where we're supposed to go next?"

Dr. Wright let out a noise somewhere between a frustrated rumble and a weary sigh. "Come with me."

They followed the director through the Hall of Fossils and into the very heart of the Hall of Cultural Artifacts. They stopped in front of an exhibit that Asha and Alex both knew well: the Nabataean Zodiac.

Hanging on the wall was a large, intricately carved stone wheel, its sharp angles worn down by centuries in the sands of the Middle East. At even intervals along the perimeter of the circle were twelve sculptures corresponding to the twelve signs of the zodiac. Most of the sculptures were detailed animal figures. Asha admired the faint scales on the fish representing Pisces. Without meaning to, Alex found himself mirroring the snarl of the Leo lion.

From previous visits to the museum, Asha remembered that the Nabataean Zodiac was named after its creators, the same people who had built the great stone city of Petra in Jordan. The wheel had deep cracks across its face. It had been discovered in pieces and brought to the museum in a large sandstone chest, which now sat on the floor beneath the rest of the exhibit. The heavy lid of the chest featured a relief sculpture of a camel. In any other context, the camel chest alone would have been enough to capture the interest of both Alex and Asha, but it paled in comparison to the cryptic zodiac.

"The signs of the zodiac are all constellations, right?" Alex asked, still staring down the stone lion.

"The Nabataeans were interested in the movements of the stars and other celestial bodies," Dr. Wright replied. "A zodiac wheel is a visual representation of those patterns. This one is a work of art, but it's also a bit like a calendar or an almanac."

"Does it predict solar eclipses?" asked Asha, recalling the eclipse that had darkened the sky on the day Dr. Fairfleet went missing.

"Does it predict the end of the world?" asked Alex, preoccupied with greater mysteries.

"Not to my knowledge," the curator said in response to both of their questions. He noticed Alex's disappointment and added, "Don't look so glum. The Zodiac is priceless. It's an important piece of our collection—possibly my favorite exhibit in the museum."

"Why's that?" Asha was more curious than disappointed. She didn't need doomsday predictions to feel the magic of the Zodiac in the dim light.

"I like to think that every artifact tells many stories—the story of its creation, the story of its use, and the story of its discovery. The Nabataean Zodiac gives us some insight, however mysterious, into the cultural practices and beliefs of a two-thousand-year-old civilization. I am also particularly fond of the story of its discovery."

Asha and Alex waited expectantly. Dr. Wright clasped his hands behind his back and began the narrative as though delivering a lecture to his undergraduate students.

"In the 1920s, archaeology was flashy and fashionable." It was clear from Dr. Wright's tone that he disapproved of both adjectives. "It was the decade that saw the discovery of King Tutankhamun's tomb in Egypt, after all. Suddenly archaeologists were celebrities, and everyone wanted to lead the next big excavation. There were longstanding rumors of ancient ruins in what was then the Emirate of Transjordan. A site to rival Petra, they said, lost to time in the desert. Museums and universities from around the world sent representatives to the region. For a few years, there was something of an archaeological race in Transjordan."

"Who won the race?" Alex asked.

"No one," Dr. Wright replied with a smug smile. "The opportunists and interlopers found nothing at all. Then in 1925 a group of Arab archaeologists, backed by the Department of Antiquities in Transjordan, invited some of the top scholars, curators, and archaeologists in the world to join their team. Among these giants was Xavier Fairfleet, Alistair's grandfather and a celebrated chairman of the Institute. United by a common goal and clear code of ethics, the international team began excavations. Within three months they discovered the extraordinary temple complex at Eremos."

Dr. Wright sounded as proud as if he had been a member of the archaeological team himself. "Through cooperation and international collaboration rather than selfish greed, those men were able to find and preserve a piece of humanity's cultural legacy. It has always been a point of pride for me that the Fairfleet Institute was a part of this historic excavation. And, of course, that's how we came to possess the Nabataean Zodiac in the first place."

Dr. Wright pointed to a letter written on a half sheet of yellowing paper that had been laminated and displayed below the informational placard for the exhibit. Asha read the letter out loud:

TRANS-JORDAN GOVERNMENT

DEPARTMENT OF ANTIQUITIES

JERASH

12 November 1925

Dear Dr. Xavier Fairfleet,

On behalf of the government of the Emirate of Transjordan and His Highness the Emir Abdullah, the Department of Antiquities extends its respect and sincere gratitude for your invaluable contributions to the excavation at Eremos. To commemorate this discovery, a triumph for the people of Transjordan and the citizens of all nations, we entrust the Fairfleet Institute with the care and curation of the Nabataean Camel Chest, and we offer, with our thanks, the bounty therein.

Alex leaned forward to get a better look at the letter. "What does all of this have to do with *our* Dr. Fairfleet?"

Dr. Wright's posture deflated. "Much of Alistair's personal research focused on the Ancient Near East. Thirty years ago, he went to Jordan on a two-year sabbatical to renew our professional relationship with the Jordanians and to continue the work that his grandfather started at Eremos. This was while Alistair was still in charge of the Museum of Natural History. I was named interim director in his absence."

"*While the cat's in the sandbox, the mouse gets promoted*," Asha recited.

"Dr. Fairfleet also said that *history repeats itself.*" Alex glared suspiciously at the director. "Maybe the mouse is looking for another promotion. Sort of incriminating, don't you think?"

"No, I don't think." There was an unexpected catch in Dr. Wright's voice. "Alistair himself appointed me interim curator, and he was happy enough with my performance to have me take on the role permanently when he became chairman of the Institute. I've worked tirelessly for this museum, and Alistair knows it. For all of his faults and mine, we have always had a cordial and productive relationship."

A glint of reflected light caught Asha's eye, and she bent down to examine the seam between the stone chest and the camel-carved lid. "There's something here."

Dr. Wright gently extracted the "something," which turned out to be an old photograph. He held it out for Alex and Asha to see. A middle-aged Dr. Fairfleet, his graying beard still flecked with red, stood in front of a roped-off excavation site. Several broken columns lay toppled in the sand, and a bored-looking camel sat off to one side with all four legs tucked under its body. In the background was a dramatic line of cliffs and a temple edifice carved into the face of the rock.

Dr. Fairfleet was smiling in the photograph, but Asha didn't think his eyes looked happy. The picture was captioned at the bottom with another couplet:

> *Goddess of wisdom and strategy too,*
> *my greatest regret is giving up you.*

"This must be the last clue," Alex guessed. "It's different, with the picture and everything."

Asha's fingers hovered over the image. "Athena was the Greek goddess of wisdom and strategy." Like any good bookworm, she knew her Greek mythology cold.

"The Nabataeans were influenced by Greek culture, so the clue could be about her."

"The Museum of Natural History used to house the bust of Pallas Athena—a rather impressive piece from classical Athens," Dr. Wright told them. "But it was moved to the Museum of Art near the start of my time as curator."

"That could be what Dr. Fairfleet means when he says that he regrets letting her go," Alex offered.

"I doubt it," Dr. Wright said, conveying very little doubt. "The Museum of Art is still part of the Fairfleet Institute. Alistair had his reasons for moving the bust, and I can assure you that 'letting go' was not among them."

"What do you mean?" Asha asked.

Dr. Wright tensed and shook his head. "Never mind. I shouldn't have brought up the bust in the first place. I don't see how it could be relevant."

Alex and Asha shared a knowing look. Dr. Wright's backpedaling was highly suspicious, and they had both read enough mystery novels to know that ancient busts were perfect hiding places for other secrets.

"May we keep this?" Asha asked, taking the photograph with both hands.

"If you like." Dr. Wright checked the lid of the camel chest one last time to make sure it hadn't been displaced or damaged. "I have no use for it."

Asha tucked the photograph between two blank pages in her notebook. "Thank you, Dr. Wright. You've been most helpful this afternoon."

"But we might have more questions for you soon. So don't try to skip town." Alex had always wanted to say that.

Dr. Wright's stony stare would have cowed a lesser detective. "I have no intention of skipping anywhere, Mr. Foster." He adjusted the lapels on his jacket, then added as if he didn't particularly care, "Where will your sleuthing take you next?"

"The art museum," Alex and Asha said together.

"We'll go as soon as it opens on Tuesday," Alex explained. "Right now I have to get home. It's pizza and movie night at my house. Should I call my mom and tell her you're coming, Asha?"

"No thanks." Asha patted her notebook. "I have some thinking to do."

"When you head to the Museum of Art, give Prudence Ito my best, won't you?" Dr. Wright's lips twitched. "That's the only part of this whole business that gives me any pleasure—imagining how annoyed poor Prudence must be."

Dr. Wright bade them a stiff goodbye and walked back to his office, his footsteps echoing in the empty museum. Asha and Alex wandered toward the exit. They paused now and then to look at various artifacts and exhibits, vestiges of the past enshrined in a dusty temple.

Outside in the warmth of the late afternoon, Asha lingered on the wide granite steps of the museum. Part of their conversation with Dr. Wright had been hovering at the back of her mind all afternoon. His words buzzed in her brain like summer flies, fat and slow but persistent. Asha sat down on the steps, took out her notebook, and flipped to the very first page on which she had written down the list of suspects in Dr. Fairfleet's disappearance. She carefully printed a fifth name at the bottom of the list:

Dr. Alistair Fairfleet

CHAPTER 3

LA GRENOUILLE DE L'ÉTANG

Tuesday, July 4ᵗʰ

The bust of Pallas Athena sat atop a pedestal in the central atrium of the Fairfleet Museum of Art. Larger than life, the goddess greeted visitors with haughty marble silence from beneath the visor of her bronze war helmet.

Alex and Asha scrutinized the bust from a safe distance, careful not to lean too far over the guard ropes around her supporting column. Every so often a visitor would pass through, and the pair of detectives would feign boredom, looking at their phones and yawning as though waiting for their parents to finish up in the museum.

After a little old lady walked by, clicking her tongue at their lack of manners, Alex positioned himself in front of the bust so that he was face-to-face with the goddess.

"I'm going to poke it," he declared.

"What? Why?" Asha knew that for every two or three stupid ideas Alex had, he would usually come up with one brilliant idea. Sometimes it was best to let him work through the duds on his own. That said, she wasn't sure she could condone the poking of a priceless work of art.

"There might be a secret compartment that opens when you press in just the right spot."

"Well, when you find 'just the right spot,' we can talk about it."

"No time." Alex's fingers twitched ominously. "Fortune favors the bold."

Alex's pointer finger made a calculated homing circle before landing on Athena's nose. No secret compartment slid open. But, as it turned out, poking the statue was not without effect.

"What *are* you doing?" The voice from across the room was clear and cutting. "Animals and unchaperoned children are not allowed in my museum. Unless you'd like to be escorted out by security, I suggest you behave like civilized adults."

Alex spun around. Dr. Prudence Ito paused at the entrance to the atrium to make sure she had been heard and understood. The museum director was as sleek and sophisticated as a modern sculpture. Her straight black hair was laced with silver. Neither Alex nor Asha knew the first thing about good style, but it was clear that this woman had it. Every piece of clothing she wore, from her pointy-toed heels to her simple jewelry to her blue patterned silk scarf, looked purposeful and expensive.

"Good morning, Dr. Ito," Asha said. "I guess you know why we're here?"

"Yes, yes. We all know what we all know. When Minnie informed the directors that you were looking for Alistair, I was hoping you would come by to make yourselves useful—not to disturb my gallery."

Alex drew himself up self-righteously. "We didn't come to be *useful*. We came to find the truth. And if that requires a little disturbance, so be it."

"Though to be clear," Asha added with a sidelong glance at her partner, who needed to tone it down a bit, "we're not against being useful if we get some information out of it as well."

"I'm not sure what information you intend to glean from prodding the centerpiece of our sculpture collection."

"We thought there might be a secret compartment," said Alex.

Dr. Ito folded her arms and tapped a finger against her elbow. "Who put that idea in your head?"

"We put ideas in our own heads," Alex retorted. "What can you tell us about the statue?"

Dr. Ito took a step back to consider the full scale of the bust. "Bust of Pallas Athena in marble and bronze. Classical Athens, fourth-century BC."

"Who sculpted it?" asked Asha.

"The most prolific artist in history: unknown." Dr. Ito sniffed at her own joke and then clarified, "For a piece like this one that was rediscovered during the Renaissance, we'll probably never know. The Museum of Art doesn't have an antiquities wing. I prefer to curate pieces whose provenance can be easily traced."

"Provenance?" Asha whipped out her notebook and prepared to take down a new definition.

"The origins and chain of ownership of a piece of art or artifact. Knowing the provenance of a piece helps to ensure that it came to the museum ethically and that it's not a fake or a forgery."

Dr. Ito must have seen Alex's eyes light up at the mention of forgery because she quickly added, "The bust of

Athena is real. She has been dated and authenticated. She's also a goddess-sized headache. I would hand her back over to John Wright and the Museum of Natural History in a heartbeat."

"Why is she a headache? Does Dr. Wright feel the same way?" Alex prodded.

"Never mind that now." It did not escape Asha's notice that Dr. Ito's evasive response sounded so much like Dr. Wright's. The art director continued, "Why are you interested in the bust in the first place?"

"We found a clue from Dr. Fairfleet in the Museum of Natural History that points to Athena." Asha closed her notebook and put it away. "And we were wondering if we could see your clue as well."

"By all means. Come with me. You aren't to touch anything without permission, though. I shouldn't have thought that needed saying, but here we are." Dr. Ito turned to leave the atrium. Asha and Alex scrambled to follow her. Before departing, Alex gave the bust of Athena an apologetic pat—discreetly, so as not to risk the displeasure of the art director.

They walked through a small gallery of Renaissance Madonnas, all with benevolent smiles and golden halos, and Dr. Ito led them up a staircase to the administrative second floor. The decor in Dr. Ito's office was modern and monochromatic. A small fountain burbled in one corner as water trickled over layered shingles of slate. Instead of a desk, there was a low glass table in the center of the room, and on the transparent tabletop were the scattered pieces of a jigsaw puzzle.

"That," said Dr. Ito with an exasperated wave of her hand, "is my clue from Alistair."

Alex was horrified. "*That* is a jigsaw puzzle. It is, by definition, a waste of time."

"I agree with you. And since my time is worth considerably more than yours, I thought I'd make the most efficient use of the available resources by having you two finish it while I get some actual work done."

"Absolutely not." Alex suppressed a childish urge to stomp his foot and instead made a hard slicing motion with his hand. "We're detectives. This isn't our sort of game."

"Speak for yourself." Asha had already parked herself cross-legged in front of the low table and was inspecting the knobby pieces of cardboard. "I love puzzles."

Alex looked at Asha with a mixture of shock and disgust, as though she had just announced that she was the spawn of alien royalty. "Nobody loves puzzles."

Asha shrugged as she fit two purple edge pieces together with a satisfying snap.

"Excellent." Dr. Ito gave a sharp nod. "It looks like the two of you have this under control. I'll make you some tea, shall I?"

Alex liked tea about as much as he liked jigsaw puzzles. He sat down next to Asha with a sullen sigh and halfheartedly tried to jam together two blue pieces that obviously were not a match.

Making tea must not have been at the top of Dr. Ito's actual to-do list because it was a full half hour before she returned with a digital tablet rather than a teapot in hand. To Asha, engrossed in the art of puzzling, it felt like five minutes. To Alex, who was less engrossed and who also had an excellent internal clock, it felt like a half hour.

Dr. Ito set her tablet on a side table and eyed the progress that Alex and Asha—primarily Asha—had made. The puzzle was far from complete, but the border was nearly finished and there were a few patches of swirling color.

"Ah." Dr. Ito arched a slender eyebrow. "I should have known. You can stop now."

"Finally!" Alex threw the handful of pieces he was holding up in the air. They rained down on the glass table like chunky confetti.

"But we're not even halfway done yet." Asha looked wistfully at the almost-finished border.

"It doesn't matter. I can see what it's meant to be."

"How?"

"I recognize that blue bit. And I have a sneaking suspicion about Alistair's motives. I'll show you, if you like."

Dr. Ito led them through the administrative hallway and down a different staircase into the modern art wing of the museum. Large, white, and brightly lit, the room made Alex feel as though he were floating in a blank sea. The paintings and sculptures, colorful as coral and shapeless as jellyfish, only added to the illusion.

Dr. Ito stopped in front of a large painting that was isolated and illuminated on its own wall. She ushered them before the painting and declared, *"La Grenouille de l'étang."*

"Bless you," said Alex.

Dr. Ito pretended not to have heard him. "Also known as *The Pond Frog*, this painting is quite possibly the most famous piece in the Fairfleet collection. Only our Rembrandt and the bust of Athena that Mr. Foster was manhandling earlier come anywhere close."

Asha could not see the frog at first, but as she looked more closely, the green, blue, and pink shapes formed themselves into a pond full of lily pads and a gaping frog mouth with a twirl of red for a tongue.

"Why's it so famous?" she asked.

"Oh, that's a question with a hundred answers and with no answer at all," Dr. Ito replied. "The artist is known as Le Merle, the Blackbird. No one knows his real name. He was one of the world's most celebrated contemporary artists in the second half of the twentieth century, but he never once appeared in public, and there are only twenty or so of his paintings in museums. The legend lives on, though the artist is now presumed dead." She eyed the painting with mild disdain. "Much of Le Merle's appeal, I believe, comes from the aura of mystery around his identity. The artwork itself is . . . derivative, in my professional opinion."

"You don't like it?"

"I don't think it's worth the fuss. But it brings visitors, and visitors bring money, and money helps us fund other exhibits. That's something, I suppose."

"Well, I like it," proclaimed Alex, who had been looking at the painting so intently that he almost seemed to be *watching* it. "The colors sort of grab you."

Dr. Ito regarded Alex with interest, as though he had said something perceptive and not, as Asha thought, something rather stupid.

"Yes, the use of color is compelling. I've always found that to be Le Merle's saving grace. Do you like art, Mr. Foster?"

"Sure, some art." Alex thought about it. "Most art, I guess."

"Do you create art?"

"I like to draw, and I like computers. I've started making some digital art."

"He's pretty good," Asha said, partially because it was true and partially because she was feeling left out of the conversation.

"You should bring your work to the museum sometime. I'd like to take a look. We have several programs for young artists and talented youth."

Alex flushed as pink as the lilies in the painting. "I don't really think of myself as an artist."

"He doesn't really think of himself as a youth, either," Asha teased.

"Well, consider it a standing offer." Dr. Ito turned her attention back to *The Pond Frog*. "Now, why did Alistair point me toward Madame Grenouille?"

"Maybe he left us a message that can only be seen under black light." If Asha strained her eyes, she could almost convince herself that there were lines of invisible text.

"I believe you've read one too many trashy art mysteries, Miss Singh."

"She's read at least twenty too many trashy art mysteries." Alex smirked, glad to be able to land a barb. Their running scorecard had been skewed heavily toward Asha of late.

"At any rate," Dr. Ito said, "I can't believe Alistair would dare mark up this painting, even with invisible ink. That's not really his style."

"What about an envelope stuck behind the painting? Is that Dr. Fairfleet's style?" Alex pointed at the top right corner of the painting. Sure enough, a cream-colored edge poked out from behind the frame.

Dr. Ito reached for the envelope, but Alex was quicker. He snatched it out from behind the painting and began to tear into the top.

"Hand over the letter, Mr. Foster. You may see its contents if—and only if—I deem it appropriate." The warning in Dr. Ito's words could not have been clearer, but Alex chose to ignore the caution tape.

"Why? What do you have to hide?" Alex glared back at the director. He began to widen the tear in the envelope.

Dr. Ito glanced at the ground. "That's interesting."

Alex paused. "What's interesting?"

"I do believe your shoelace is untied."

Alex looked down for only a second, but a second was all it took. Dr. Ito's hand shot out and plucked the envelope right out of his grasp.

Alex and Asha both gaped at the museum director. Neither of them could believe that Dr. Ito had used a ruse as transparent as the old shoelace trick. And neither of them could believe that it had worked.

Indifferent to their indignation, Dr. Ito finished tearing open the envelope. The two young detectives tried to get a glimpse of its contents. They both managed a quick peek before Dr. Ito stepped back, pulling the piece of paper closer to her chest.

This is what Alex saw: a photocopy of one of Dr. Ito's checks made out for $5,000 and signed by the director herself in neat, elegant cursive. The "Pay to the Order of" field and the "Date" field were both blank.

Dr. Prudence Ito The Fairfleet Museum of Art	1025
	DATE
PAY TO THE ORDER OF	$ *5,000.00*
Five Thousand and 00/100	DOLLARS
MEMO	*Prudence Ito*

64

This is what Asha saw: a printout of a bank statement with four $5,000 deposits dated December 1st, February 1st, April 1st, and June 1st. Asha was unable to glimpse the name on the bank statement, and so she had no idea whom Dr. Ito was referring to when the director sucked in a breath through her teeth and hissed, "That little worm!"

Dr. Ito crumpled the sheet of paper in her white-knuckled fist. "If you children will excuse me, I've some business to attend to." Her anger did not roar or crackle; it burned hot blue. "I trust you can see yourselves out." And with that, Dr. Ito marched out of the modern art wing, heels clacking on the marble floor.

Asha and Alex waited until she was just out of sight and then hurried after her, trailing at a safe distance. They followed her as far as the parking lot but were forced to concede defeat when she got into a silver Mercedes and drove away. Not having a driver's license could be a real disadvantage in the detective business.

With much to mull over, they snuck past reception back into the museum and spent some time looking at *La Grenouille de l'étang* for any hints they might have missed.

Asha wanted to return to the administrative wing. "I think Dr. Ito left her office unlocked," she said. "We should take the puzzle."

Alex grimaced. "Why? Dr. Ito already figured out her clue."

"Then she won't mind if we bag the evidence."

In the end, it was the chance to snoop around Dr. Ito's office—and not the possibility of more puzzle time—that persuaded Alex. But when they retraced their path through the modern art wing to the administrative staircase, they discovered an unexpected obstacle: an elderly museum guard, whose name tag simply said FRED, was seated next to the door.

It was clear to both Alex and Asha that this was the sort of guard who had been hired to point visitors kindly toward the restroom and not, say, to chase down art burglars during a heist. In the nearly empty museum, he sat snoozing in his chair. Whenever he exhaled, each breath just short of a snore, his gray mustache fluttered above his upper lip.

"What now?" Asha whispered. As helpful as Fred looked, she didn't think he would let them just waltz into Dr. Ito's office.

"He's out cold." Alex waved his arms and did a silent, taunting jig. "I bet we can make it past him."

Asha knew how much noise Alex Foster could make when he was trying to be quiet. "Maybe I should go first."

She tiptoed in a wide arc, skirting an abstract bronze sculpture in the center of the room. The polished floor in the modern art wing was flat and forgiving; no creaking boards threatened to give her away. When she was mere feet from the guard, she held her breath and reached for the door handle, which yielded with a soft click. Fred's eyes shot open.

"And just where do you think you're going, miss?"

Asha jumped back as though the handle had burned her palm. "I—I was—" she stammered. "Dr. Ito's office?"

Fred's eyes narrowed and his mustache bristled. "Dr. Ito has left for the day." He stood up creakily, bracing himself against his chair. "Why don't you head along home now too. The museum's closing soon."

Asha mumbled an unconvincing apology and retreated to rejoin Alex behind the bronze statue. "New plan," she whispered. "Quiet didn't work out, so I'm going to need you to make as much noise as possible. Distract *Fred* so I can get past him."

Alex grinned. Loud, he could do. He rummaged around in his pockets and took out a handful of bang snap firecrackers, a neon green whistle, and a quarter.

"Why are you carrying all of that around?" Asha asked, marveling at the motley assortment.

Alex shrugged. "It's the Fourth of July."

He scanned the galleries, wondering where to stage his own masterpiece. Most of the art wings had dull, muffled acoustics. What he really needed was a good echo . . .

"Right. You stay here!" Alex knew what he had to do. He took off running while Asha flattened herself against the nearest wall, waiting for her opening. Alex didn't stop until he reached the central atrium with the bust of Athena. The ceiling was high and domed, and the squeak of his sneakers reverberated loudly in the empty chamber.

With barely contained anticipation, Alex held up one of the firecrackers. Pallas Athena watched him from her pedestal, her fierce eyes daring him to proceed.

"If you insist," Alex said. And proceed he did.

Back in the modern art wing, Asha heard a cacophony of pops, cracks, and bangs followed by three shrill whistle blasts and, at the very end of it all, the clatter of a quarter dropping onto a marble floor.

A moment later, Fred hobbled past her, running as fast as his stiff legs would carry him. When the mustachioed guard was safely out of sight, Asha crept back through the gallery and slipped into the administrative wing. The rest of her expedition was free from obstacles. The carpet muffled her footsteps in the deserted corridor, and Dr. Ito's office was indeed unlocked. She swept the puzzle pieces off the glass table and into her backpack, then gave the room a quick once-over to make sure everything was in order. The slate fountain gurgled conspiratorially in the corner.

Asha found Alex sitting outside on the steps of the art museum, where he had been banished by an angry Fred. He looked very pleased with himself—probably because he was very pleased with himself. As they walked home in the glaring afternoon sun, the detectives were finally at liberty to discuss what they'd discovered in the museum.

"So, we agree there's something Dr. Wright and Dr. Ito are both hiding about the bust of Athena. *La Grenouille de l'étang* is fishy . . . er, froggy . . . as well. And Dr. Ito has been paying someone off with five-thousand-dollar checks, but she didn't know who," Asha summarized.

"And when she found out, she was mad. Really mad."

"All of that seems to add up to blackmail to me."

"That piece of paper practically reeked of blackmail," Alex agreed. He wondered what blackmail would smell like in a literal way. Like slimy, rotten vegetables, maybe. Or like the dark gunk in sink drains. "But then who has been blackmailing Dr. Ito? And why?"

"The whole thing is suspicious. Dr. Fairfleet clearly knew about whatever Dr. Ito's been hiding. Maybe that made him a target."

"Nah." Alex scuffed the toe of his sneaker against the pavement. "It's more likely Dr. Ito is one of the people that Dr. Fairfleet described as 'sharing a secret' in his letter. She's hiding something, but I think she's one of the good guys."

"You like her," Asha observed. "Even though she got you with that shoelace trick?"

Alex shook his head, half in disbelief and half in admiration. "She caught me off guard. It won't happen again."

On the evening of the Fourth of July, the Singhs and the Fosters went to Pendleton Park for Northbrook's annual fireworks. Little Ollie babbled on their picnic blanket, tugging on patient old Donkey's ears. Asha liked watching the other families as they chatted and shared Tupperware containers of homemade brownies and watermelon cubes with their neighbors. Alex, who believed that the truest form of American patriotism was rebellion against authority, was not entirely sold on the spirit of the Fourth of July, but he also wasn't above enjoying a good pyrotechnics display. The high school band played cymbal-crashing marches in the band shell as the sky exploded with bursts of red, white, and purple-blue.

Later that night, Asha stayed up until one in the morning finishing the puzzle they had taken from Dr. Ito's office. After the fact, she would argue that she had a strange sixth sense about the puzzle—that she knew it would yield a clue. In truth, she couldn't bear to leave a jigsaw puzzle unfinished.

When the puzzle was complete, she took a picture with her phone, her heart beating with the thrill of discovery. It was indeed *La Grenouille de l'étang* in all her amphibian glory, but on the largest lily pad was something unexpected: a message written in a dark blue, loopy script.

"Jesters do oft prove prophets." –5

A quick internet search confirmed Asha's suspicion about the source. She sent Alex the picture followed by a short message:

> King Lear. Act 5, Scene 3.

Alex must have been burning the midnight oil himself because he replied less than a minute later:

> Coincidence? I think not.

Alex's message contained a link that took Asha to the audition notification page for the Fairfleet Center for the Performing Arts.

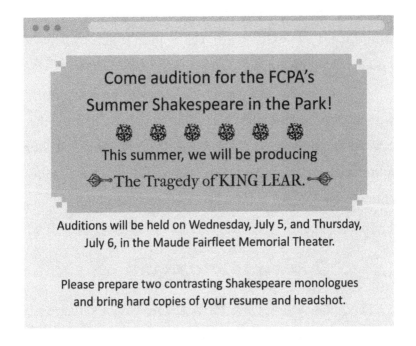

Come audition for the FCPA's
Summer Shakespeare in the Park!

This summer, we will be producing
The Tragedy of KING LEAR.

Auditions will be held on Wednesday, July 5, and Thursday, July 6, in the Maude Fairfleet Memorial Theater.

Please prepare two contrasting Shakespeare monologues and bring hard copies of your resume and headshot.

Asha sent Alex one last message before hopping into bed and burying her head in her pillows. She wasn't at all sleepy, but the sooner she could force herself to fall asleep, the sooner it would be morning, and the sooner they could be back on the case.

Prep your monologues. It looks like we're headed to the theater tomorrow.

CHAPTER 4

DRAMATIC ACTION

Wednesday, July 5th

The mainstage theater at the Fairfleet Center for the Performing Arts was hot and stuffy despite recent renovations to its air-conditioning system. The dusty warmth combined with the low lighting made it hard for Alex to keep from drifting off. The Shakespeare monologues weren't helping.

Asha and Alex had walked into the empty theater and taken seats a few rows behind Quentin Carlisle and his assistant. The young detectives didn't bother asking permission to observe the auditions. They had discovered long ago that two children on a college campus could go almost anywhere; as long as they weren't disruptive, most adults would assume they were faculty kids waiting for their parents.

A bewhiskered old man shuffled out to the center of the stage for his audition. Quentin Carlisle riffled through the headshots in front of him. "Whenever you're ready, Mr. Ellsworth."

The man coughed and spluttered to clear his throat, then drew himself up with a theatrical inhalation. "To BE, or not to BE," he began, before breaking into another coughing fit.

"Why's he saying it like that?" Asha asked Alex under her breath.

Apparently, her remarks weren't quite under her breath enough because it was Quentin Carlisle who responded, "That *is* the question." The director of the FCPA tapped his papers into a stack and stood up briskly. "Go get a drink of water, Mr. Ellsworth. We'll pick back up in ten."

Carlisle passed the stack of resumes and headshots to his assistant, who scurried off without a word. Picking up a coffee mug from his director's table, he started toward the back of the theater. "You two—Nancy Drew and Drew

Nancy—come with me." He did not look to see if Alex and Asha followed him.

Quentin Carlisle's office was a cramped room behind the theater's box office. The walls were covered in pictures of Carlisle with famous actors who had taken on guest roles at the theater. There were no bookshelves, but piles of scripts and scores filled the corners and lined the walls.

Carlisle slumped in the chair behind his desk and surveyed the young detectives with the unimpressed gaze of a casting director. Alex and Asha surveyed him right back, equally unimpressed. Carlisle was not a large man, but he cut a handsome figure. Dark hair. Angular features. Only his pale complexion and a bit of red around his eyes suggested that he might be fraying under the stress of current circumstances. He was wearing two pieces of a three-piece suit—high quality but rumpled, as though he had slept in them.

"So, what can I do for the A&A Detective Agency?" Carlisle's voice was crisp and curt, with an actor's precise articulation.

Alex placed both hands on the desk and leaned forward dramatically. Drama, he decided, was the only language these theater people understood. "Tell us about *King Lear*."

Whatever Carlisle had been expecting them to open with, it clearly wasn't that. He made a sour face and took a sip from his coffee mug. "What do you want to discuss? Themes? Dramaturgy? Historical basis?"

"We'd settle for knowing about this particular production," Alex replied.

Carlisle shrugged. "It's Shakespeare in the Park. We stage a production every summer, just as they do in every town in America that has green space and a few wealthy donors. We're not talking revolutionary theater here."

"But why *King Lear*?" Asha asked, tugging on Alex's shirt to pull him back into his chair. "Was it your choice?"

"Now that you mention it, *Lear* was poor old Alistair's idea. I would have chosen a comedy—*Midsummer, As You Like It*—something crowd-pleasing. But Alistair pushed for *Lear*."

"Do you know if *King Lear* has any personal significance for him?" Asha pressed. "Our evidence suggests the play may have something to do with his disappearance."

Quentin Carlisle adjusted his rumpled vest. "Not that I know of." He paused, then smirked. "Unless you mean that the old geezer lost his marbles and wandered off into the heath. That might be the best theory I've heard yet."

"What's a heath?" Alex asked.

"The heath is . . . well, heathland." Carlisle cast around for an easy definition. "The wild, shrubby meadows of England." He proceeded to quote grandly: "'Now would I give a thousand furlongs of sea for an acre of barren ground, long heath, brown furze . . .'"

"What? Furs?" Talking to Quentin Carlisle made Alex feel like he had a sharp popcorn husk stuck in his gums. "This is an investigation! Speak English!"

"Easy now." The director flashed his perfect teeth. "I'm just answering your questions. Take a deep breath, Sherlock."

"Don't tell me what to do!" Alex spat back. "And don't call me Sherlock."

Carlisle seemed to enjoy Alex's frustration. "As this is your first real case, maybe I can help you with the interrogation. Ask me if I had anything to do with Alistair Fairfleet's disappearance."

"Well, did you?"

"I'm sorry. Did I what?"

Alex fumed. "Have anything to do with Dr. Fairfleet's disappearance?"

Carlisle took a loud, slurping sip of his coffee. "No. Now ask me if I know anything about the missing charter."

"Do you know anything about the missing charter?" Alex asked through gritted teeth.

"No."

"So, what, then? You're just wasting our time?"

Carlisle looked at Alex over the lip of his mug. "As you are wasting mine."

Alex rounded on Asha. "You're being awfully quiet. Why aren't you helping?"

Asha was, in fact, feeling a tad queasy. She tried to keep her voice steady as she asked, "What did you mean when you said that Dr. Fairfleet might be losing his mind?"

Carlisle seemed taken aback by Asha's question and by the frank concern on her face. "It was a joke, that's all," he replied. "King Lear's descent into madness is the driving force behind the conflict of the play. Poor Alistair is well past his prime. Now he's gone off and left us all these absurd clues. Life imitates art, you know."

The churning in Asha's stomach intensified. She avoided Alex's questioning gaze.

Alex turned his attention back to Carlisle. "Speaking of clues," he said, "have you solved yours yet?"

A flash of irritation, mean and nasty, crossed Quentin Carlisle's face. "No, I haven't."

"Can we see it? Maybe we can help."

"Absolutely not."

Alex tried once more to catch Asha's eye, a little resentfully now. He hadn't expected to carry out the entire interrogation on his own. Alex stumbled into his next question. "But . . . I mean . . . why not?"

Quentin Carlisle wore a snakelike smile now that he had the upper hand again. "There are so many answers to that question, but I'll give you two. First, you are ten years old. And second, I don't want to."

Alex's ears turned a dangerous shade of red. "You think we're *ten*?" he demanded. "And what sort of response is '*I don't want to*'? Do you have any idea how suspicious that makes you sound?"

Carlisle fed off Alex's anger, growing cooler and more composed as the young detective grew more upset. "To be honest, it doesn't really bother me if Mini Miss Marple and Hercule Poirot Jr. find me suspicious."

Asha started running through the ways that she could stop her partner from punching a grown man who, though relatively small, was still much larger than Alex. She was saved from having to act by Carlisle's assistant, who knocked tentatively before poking her head into the office.

"Mr. Carlisle, the actors are waiting."

"Thank you, Janet." Quentin Carlisle stood up and pushed a stack of papers toward the edge of his desk. "These scripts need to be sorted out before the read-through tomorrow. You won't mind staying late tonight."

Janet did not bother responding to this non-question. She accepted the stack of scripts and retreated to a spindly chair in the corner. Carlisle looked at Asha and Alex and made an exaggerated gesture toward the door. "And that, as we say in the business, is your cue, gumshoes."

"But you didn't tell us anything useful!" Alex grumbled.

"Them's the breaks."

Carlisle steered them out into the hallway, shut his office door, and straightened his vest again. "Cheers. Thanks so much for coming. Let's *not* do this again." He strolled back to the auditorium with a lazy indifference that offended Alex greatly.

Alex and Asha stood in the hall, more than a little nettled. "What was that all about?" Alex asked. "Something Carlisle said really got to you."

"You think he really got to *me*?" Asha scoffed.

"All right, so he got to both of us. What did he say that upset you so much?"

Asha leaned against the wall and looked down at her feet. "Do you remember last summer when we were starting up the agency, and Dr. Fairfleet kept forgetting the names of the authors he wanted us to read? He would always get flustered about it."

"I guess so. I mean, he's pretty old, Asha."

"I know. That's how it started with my Nani. At first she would forget words and names and things like that, but eventually she couldn't even remember who I was."

"You think that Dr. Fairfleet is losing his memory? That he has dementia or something?"

"We ignored Dr. Wright's explanation because we couldn't see what motive Dr. Fairfleet would have in his own disappearance, but what if there *is* no motive? What if he's confused? Or worse, lost?"

"Nope, no way," Alex said, rocking back and forth in his sneakers. "He can't be confused. He left everyone these complicated riddles. And the letter says that one of the directors is responsible for his disappearance. If you ask me, this jerk Carlisle is probably behind the whole thing, and he's just trying to throw us off the scent."

Asha took a deep, shaky breath. "You're right. We need to get Carlisle's clue."

Alex inched forward to peek through the narrow window in the office door. Janet the assistant was still seated in her rickety chair, poring over the stack of scripts with a highlighter in hand.

He tried the door handle, to no avail. "The door must lock when it shuts. Do you have a hairpin?"

Asha resisted the urge to roll her eyes. She failed. "No one has hairpins anymore. And even if I did, there's not a chance you would be able to pick that lock."

"You don't know that," Alex argued. "I've seen it done in movies loads of times. How hard can it be?"

"Hard enough to keep out a couple of kids who don't even have a hairpin, I expect. Anyway, unlocking the door doesn't solve the Janet problem."

Alex considered their options. "What if we knock on the door and tell Janet that Carlisle needs her to run an errand? Say that he yelled at us. I bet she'd believe you if you cried a little."

He didn't even need to look at his partner's face to know that this plan would never fly. Asha was neither a liar nor a crier. He admired her for that, even when it made their job harder. "Look," Alex said, "I get it if you don't want to take the low road, but you'd better find an alternative high road soon."

Asha fiddled with the strap of her backpack. While a detective needed a moral code, she knew that they also needed to be willing to take necessary risks. Caution was one thing; cowardice was another. She refused to give in to the latter. "I might have an idea."

"Let's hear it!"

"Your diversion at the Museum of Art yesterday worked great."

Alex turned out his pockets. "Too bad I'm out of firecrackers."

"I might be able to buy us even more time than that." Asha pointed to the end of the hallway. On the far wall was a square of recognizable red: a fire alarm pull station.

When Alex caught her drift, he beamed with delight. "That's perfect! You pull the alarm. I'll wait here and catch the door when Janet leaves."

Asha's audacity wavered. "What if you pull the alarm and I catch the door?"

Alex was tempted—she could see it in his mischief-bright eyes—but he shook his head. "This is your plan. You should do the honors."

She knew he was right.

The hallway, that last distance between Asha and a potentially terrible choice, was shorter than it appeared. She paused at the end of the hall with her fingertips on the lever to consider the kind of children who generally pulled fire alarms: pranksters and delinquents and people with no concern for actual fire safety.

And, she concluded, intrepid detectives. Asha took a deep breath and pulled the alarm.

Pressed against the wall near the door to Carlisle's office, Alex was prepared for the wailing sirens to go off. He was less prepared for Janet, who charged out of the office and toward the prop department, wielding a small fire extinguisher like a battle weapon. He was so surprised to see the shy assistant in action that he nearly failed to catch the door when it bounced off the rubber stop.

Asha, on the other hand, was laser focused. Her act of defiance would not be in vain. She sprinted down the hallway and lunged for the narrowing gap. Both detectives caught hold of the door just before it locked on them for good.

Hearts drumming, they slipped into Carlisle's office and shut the door behind them so that the blare of the alarm in the hall was less distracting. It took them only a minute or so of searching to determine where Carlisle must have hidden his clue. The top drawer of the desk was locked, and there was no key in sight.

On the desk was a little dish containing an assortment of the director's personal items, including—of all things—a silver tiepin. Alex held up the pin, which glinted in the light. A flickering ball of excitement expanded in his chest. It was fate. Destiny.

Asha saw the expression on his face and suppressed a laugh. "Oh, go ahead, then," she said. "But hurry up. We don't have long."

"I won't need long." Alex closed his eyes, rolling the pin between his palms. He bent down and carefully inserted the silver needle into the lock. After several seconds of jostling, Alex felt the lock give way with a click. Both detectives gaped at the makeshift lockpick. Despite his apparent confidence, Alex was almost as stunned as Asha.

Alex slid open the drawer and inspected its contents: a fancy bottle of cologne, several credit cards, a folded sheet of Dr. Fairfleet's creamy stationery that had to be Carlisle's clue, and one other thing . . .

"Asha, look at this." Alex pointed at another piece of paper in the drawer, forcing Asha to lean over the desk to get a better look.

What they saw was a check from Dr. Prudence Ito for five thousand dollars. The "Pay to the Order of" field had Quentin Carlisle's name in the blank, filled in after the fact in different handwriting.

Alex remembered what Dr. Ito had said when she saw the name of her blackmailer on the bank statement, and he repeated her words now: "That little worm!"

"Sounds like Carlisle to me," Asha agreed. In the hallway, the fire alarm had been shut off. The silence put Asha on edge. "Take the check, and let's have a look at the clue."

Alex took out the piece of Dr. Fairfleet's signature stationery and spread it flat on the desk. Written on the paper was a short poem:

A schemer with morals most troublin'

Had scams and ambitions a-bubblin'

These crimes never pay

Better call it a day

It's five o'clock somewhere—try Dublin

Alex scratched his head. Not understanding things made him itchy. "It's definitely not Shakespeare."

"It's a limerick," Asha said. "Limerick is a place in Ireland, like Dublin."

Alex took the bottle of cologne from the drawer. He popped off the stopper and took a whiff. The smoky scent made him want to sneeze. He grimaced and put the bottle back. "If Carlisle is the one blackmailing Dr. Ito, then 'troubling morals' is kind of an understatement, don't you think?"

They didn't hear the door open, and so they were unprepared for the voice that snapped them out of their snooping, a voice low and tight with rage. "You two are very much going to regret this."

The detectives spun around to see Quentin Carlisle framed in the doorway. Alex had encountered his fair share of angry adults, but he had never seen one look quite so mean. "What are you going to do? Call the cops? We've seen the check from Dr. Ito. Your game is up, Carlisle."

"You don't have any idea what you're talking about," the director snarled. "By the time I'm done with you, you're going to wish that the police were involved."

Asha saw her own apprehension reflected in Alex's tense posture. "You realize you're threatening a couple of kids, right?" she asked.

"From what I can see, I am threatening a pair of thieves who broke into my office."

"You want it?" Alex held up the clue and crumpled the piece of stationery into a ball. "Go get it!"

Alex hurled the ball of paper into the far corner of the room. Carlisle lunged for it, abandoning his position in the doorframe, and Alex and Asha took their opportunity to bolt.

Carlisle swore, but the detectives were already out of reach. The pair sprinted down the hallway, around a corner, and out into the bright sunshine. Normally, Asha was faster than Alex, but emotions like fear and guilt tended to slow her down while they sped Alex up. At any rate, they were both faster than Quentin Carlisle.

The wind rushed through Alex's curls and Asha's hair streamed behind her as they ran. The tower of the Trinity Clock was all that could be seen of the Fairfleet Center for the Performing Arts now. Their fear faded, and soon Alex and Asha weren't running from anyone or anything but rather chasing the carefree exhilaration of a summer afternoon.

CHAPTER 5

WRONG TURNS AND RED HERRINGS

Thursday, July 6ᵗʰ

The next day, Asha and Alex parted ways to conduct their own investigations. It wasn't such an unusual strategy for the A&A Detective Agency. They could cover more ground this way, and when they had separate hunches, they sometimes needed to follow separate leads.

Asha's path led her to the neurology clinic of Dr. Ellen Price. There was only one neurologist in Northbrook—and fortunately she was a good one. A quick internet search yielded an impressive list of accolades and awards for Dr. Price's work with Alzheimer's and dementia.

For her trip to the clinic, Asha wore a crisp blouse and a neat plaid skirt. She put her long hair up in a donut-shaped bun atop her head. Asha wanted to look as grown up as possible. Despite her best efforts, however, the receptionist—a young man with kind eyes—seemed surprised to see her. Asha supposed they weren't accustomed to having children in the neurology clinic. There were no toys with colorful wooden beads in the waiting room, just magazines advertising cruises and plant-based diets.

"Excuse me," Asha addressed the receptionist. "I need to speak to Dr. Price."

"Do you have an appointment?"

"No, but I need to speak with her."

The man gave her a sympathetic smile. "I'm afraid that Dr. Price doesn't see anyone without an appointment. We can set something up if you like."

"I need to see her today. It's important. Tell her . . ." Asha weighed the risk of her next words. "Tell her it's about Dr. Fairfleet's disappearance."

Her comment had the desired effect. The receptionist's smile faded. "One moment, please." He disappeared into the back of the clinic, returning a few seconds later. "Dr. Price will see you."

The receptionist ushered Asha into Dr. Price's personal office. A tall woman in her late fifties sat at a desk, sorting through a pile of paperwork. Her hair was short and gray, and she had the face of someone who believed in delivering bad news as directly as possible.

The neurologist stood up and offered Asha her hand. "How are you? I'm Dr. Price. What's your name?"

"Asha Singh." Asha shook the doctor's hand. Her grip was strong.

Dr. Price sat back down, pulled her chair up to her desk, and folded her hands in front of her. All of her actions were precise and efficient. "Matthew informs me that you want to talk about Alistair Fairfleet. I'm sure you can appreciate that I'm not at liberty to discuss the private health concerns of my patients."

Asha felt a lump of lead form in her throat and drop all the way to the bottom of her stomach. "So Dr. Fairfleet is your patient, then?"

Dr. Price frowned. Asha wondered if the neurologist was thinking about Dr. Fairfleet or if she was annoyed that she may have been tricked into divulging more than she should have. Dr. Price did not elaborate. She said only, "I'm sorry I can't be of more help."

"But he's been missing for weeks now. Aren't you worried about him?" Asha wished she had Alex's knack for getting under the skin of a suspect or witness. She wasn't sure how to make this rational doctor open up.

"Of course I'm worried about Alistair. That's not the point."

"There must be some exceptions to the rules if you have any information that could help the police," Asha pushed back.

"First of all, you are not the police. And second of all . . ." Dr. Price hesitated, casting a quick glance at her closed office door. "Well, let me put it this way: *Hypothetically*, if a neurologist had a patient involved in a crime or a missing person's case, but the patient was at such an early stage of his disease that the doctor judged it to be irrelevant, then it would be inappropriate for the doctor to violate standard privacy practices."

"Hypothetically?" Asha echoed.

"Hypothetically," Dr. Price repeated, stressing each syllable.

"You don't know anything that could help lead us to Dr. Fairfleet?"

"I'm afraid not." The neurologist was apologetic but firm.

Asha sighed and took out an A&A Agency card. "If you think of anything, please let me know."

As Asha was leaving the clinic, the receptionist, Matthew, stopped her. "Wait a second." He waived her over to the desk. "You're Asha Singh?"

"Yes," Asha replied cautiously.

"I have something for you. From Dr. Fairfleet."

Asha wasn't sure what to make of this development. She stood there stupidly as her tongue caught up with her brain. "For me?"

Matthew reached into a drawer and pulled out a cream-colored envelope. "Dr. Fairfleet was one of my professors at Waverly College. Back in March he gave me this envelope. He told me that if anything happened to him and that if you showed up asking questions, I should give it to you." The young man tapped the corner of the envelope against the desk. "But he led me to believe there would be two of you."

"There are two of us," Asha assured him, feeling a bubbling sensation of renewed hope. "I'm part of the A&A Detective Agency. A&A stands for Asha and Alex."

Matthew held out the envelope. "Well then, good luck," he said. "Dr. Fairfleet obviously has a lot of faith in you. Bring him back for us, won't you?"

Meanwhile, at the Fairfleet Museum of Art, Alex had some questions for Dr. Prudence Ito. Unfortunately, Dr. Prudence Ito didn't seem to have time for Alex.

"It's not that I don't enjoy hearing your insights," Dr. Ito told him. Alex wasn't sure if she was being sarcastic or not. "But I have an exhibition opening next week, and with the board of trustees breathing down my neck . . ."

Alex had worked out a plan—a good one—to get Dr. Ito to give up the information he wanted. First, he would ease in with some small talk, throw a few softball questions. Then he'd add a bit of intentional misdirection before getting to the heart of the matter. However, the whole plan depended upon Dr. Ito's talking to him in the first place. Sometimes a detective had to throw away the script.

"Dr. Ito, is Quentin Carlisle blackmailing you?" Alex blurted out.

Prudence Ito took off her reading glasses and gave Alex a hard stare. "Come in, Mr. Foster. And shut the door."

Once Alex was seated next to the low glass table in Dr. Ito's office, the museum director said sternly, "I would like to know where you're getting your information."

Alex shifted with discomfort. He was on the ground while Dr. Ito was sitting on her tasteful settee, so he felt especially small, like a kindergartener facing his teacher. "We saw part of a bank statement the other day in the modern art wing. Then yesterday, we found this in Quentin Carlisle's office." Alex took the check from his pocket and handed it to her. It was slightly crumpled.

"You found it." Dr. Ito did not sound convinced. "I suppose Carlisle just left it sitting out on his desk?"

Alex suspected that this question was rhetorical, so he chose not to answer her. "It is blackmail, though, isn't it?"

Dr. Ito ripped the check into four even pieces before responding. "Blackmail is a strong accusation. I was paying Carlisle to keep his mouth shut about things he does not understand."

"Look, Dr. Ito," Alex said, trying to imitate the earnest quality that Asha had while talking to adults. He wasn't sure how she did it. Earnest was not really his style. "I think this whole thing between you and Quentin Carlisle is what Dr. Fairfleet was talking about in his letter when he said that two of the directors share a secret that needs to come out. That would mean you're *not* the one behind his disappearance. But to cross you off the suspect list, I need to know what Quentin Carlisle has on you."

"You will have to keep me on your list a bit longer then."

Dr. Ito's response showed a fundamental lack of respect for the suspect list that Alex found concerning. "I can't accept that answer."

"No?"

"I'm on your side. You're just being stubborn!"

"Oh, *I'm* being stubborn, am I?" Dr. Ito's voice was tinged with dry amusement.

Alex glared at her. "Detectives aren't stubborn—they're dogged."

"Indeed," Dr. Ito replied. Once again, Alex couldn't tell if she was agreeing with him or making fun of him or both. "You're going to have to be dogged and seek a different route if you want to follow up on this check business, I'm afraid. Though I would advise you to let it go. Is there anything else I can help you with before I get back to the very important work that you are forcing me to neglect?"

"Well, since you asked . . ." Alex had thrown away Quentin Carlisle's clue as a necessary diversion but not before he had memorized the limerick. He recited it for Dr. Ito.

When he finished, Dr. Ito let slip a single chuckle. "Sometimes I forget that Alistair can be funny," she said.

"Does it mean anything to you?" Alex asked.

"Yes and no. It seems more like an insult than a clue to me, given the reference to Dublin."

Alex perked up. "What about Dublin?"

Dr. Ito eyed Alex as if weighing how much he deserved to know. "Carlisle applied for a job at Trinity College Dublin a few years ago—a tenure-track professorship in their drama department. He got fairly far along in the process before it came out that he had forged a letter of recommendation from Alistair. He wrote the whole thing himself."

"Seriously? Why wasn't he fired?"

She gave a condescending shrug. "You can ask Alistair if you ever find him. Carlisle is very good at his job—I'll give him that much. He was an up-and-coming director in New York City before accepting his role here. And, of course, he's always been successful with our easily charmed donors. The irony is that I think Alistair would have written him an excellent recommendation for the Trinity College position if he had only asked."

Hearing the name of the college again set off chimes in Alex's sleuthing subconscious. "Does Trinity College have anything to do with the Trinity Clock on campus?"

"Oh yes, the clock was a gift from the Irish. Waverly College has a longstanding relationship with Trinity College

Dublin. We host exchange students, trade visiting profes-
sorships, that sort of thing."

Alex sprang to his feet. "Thanks, Dr. Ito! You've been
super helpful!"

Dr. Ito raised her eyebrows and put her glasses back
on. "Well, I do try." She began to peruse the papers on her
lap once more.

Alex was halfway out the door when Dr. Ito called to
him. "And Mr. Foster—next time you come to interrupt
my work, I expect to see some of your art."

Asha waited until she was alone to open the creamy envelope that Matthew had given her. It contained a single slip
of paper: an order ticket from Behrman's Delicatessen with
the number 22 scrawled on it in blue ink.

Asha knew Behrman's Deli, of course. Everybody
knew Behrman's Deli. It had been a Northbrook institution for more than a hundred years. They didn't have a
menu printed anywhere; customers had to know what the
deli served before ordering at the high counter. Those who
were really in the know could write down a number on a

ticket and Mr. Behrman—the fourth Mr. Behrman to run the deli—would take their order.

She rode her bike down Main Street, past the quaint restaurants and shops of Northbrook. Some of Asha's favorite places were on Main Street, including an independent bookstore called NorthBook and the town's only CVS.

It was midafternoon by the time she arrived at Behrman's Deli. The lunch rush had died down, but there was an old couple sharing a pastrami sandwich at a corner table. Though the deli was small, the wooden counter was impressively solid. There was a glass display case full of cured meats, various potato salads, and knishes.

Mr. Behrman himself stood behind the counter. He was a big bear of a man with bright eyes and a booming, jovial voice. When Asha gave him the order ticket, he squinted at her, then down at the ticket, then back up at her.

"Are you sure this is what you want?" he asked.

"Umm . . . yes," Asha said. "Please," she added as an afterthought.

"It'll just be a moment." Mr. Behrman took a pickle from a barrel behind the counter and handed it to Asha on a sheet of deli paper. "While you wait. On the house."

Asha munched on the pickle while Mr. Behrman stepped into the kitchen. It was crisp, sour, salty, and juicy—everything a pickle should be. A bit of pickle brine dribbled down her chin and onto her blouse.

When Mr. Behrman returned, Asha laid a ten-dollar bill on the counter and accepted the newspaper-wrapped bundle that the delicatessen owner held out for her. She peeled back a corner of the newspaper to discover three pieces of fish that had been salted and smoked until they were dry and reddish-brown. They were decidedly pungent.

Asha wrinkled her nose and pulled the newspaper back over the fragrant fish. "I'm sorry, Mr. Behrman, but what is this?"

The delicatessen owner crossed his burly arms and shook his massive head. "It's what you ordered, young lady," he said. "Number twenty-two: red herring."

Alex and Asha met up in the late afternoon at Pendleton Park, which was at the center of Waverly campus, right across the street from the Fairfleet Center for the Performing Arts. They bought frozen treats from an ice-cream truck. Asha selected a classic strawberry shortcake ice cream bar, while Alex chose a multicolored rocket-shaped Popsicle that turned his mouth bright blue. They settled down with their backs against the trunk of a giant oak tree.

"So, what did you find out?" Alex asked, loudly slurping his Popsicle.

Asha took the newspaper-wrapped packet from her backpack and handed it to him. Alex unwrapped the fish and sniffed it. "What is it?"

"A red herring," Asha replied.

"Huh." Alex tore off a piece of the fish and popped it in his mouth. It was very salty and very strong. It did not pair well with fruity Popsicle. "Dr. Fairfleet has a strange sense of humor."

"He's trying to tell us we're on the wrong track." She took a bite of her ice cream and let it melt in her mouth before adding, "The thing is, I'm not sure I was on the wrong track—maybe just an adjacent track. Dr. Fairfleet is a patient at the clinic, even if he's only in the early stages of losing his memory. And then there's *King Lear* and the whole question of his retirement. I don't think it's a coincidence."

Alex tore off another piece of herring. The second bite was better than the first.

"My trip to the neurologist wasn't a waste," Asha continued. "The man who gave me the red herring clue said that Dr. Fairfleet gave him the envelope in March, which makes me think that the letters and clues were probably planned out months in advance. Dr. Fairfleet might not have even sent them this summer. He could have set them up to be sent in the event of his disappearance."

Alex was about to ask if she really thought someone could have that much foresight, but he stopped himself. This was Dr. Fairfleet they were talking about, after all. Instead, he changed gears to tell Asha about his conversation with Dr. Ito and Quentin Carlisle's ill-fated job interview.

"Carlisle really is slimy, isn't he?" Asha remarked.

"What I don't get is how he thought he could get away with forging the letter of recommendation. He was obviously going to get caught. At least his blackmail plan had a better payoff."

Alex could tell that Asha disapproved of this last statement. The way her brow crinkled always made him feel like he had shown up to class without his homework. He hated that feeling.

"Both of those things were wrong," she said. "Forging the letter wouldn't be any less wrong if Carlisle had gotten away with it."

"That's not what I meant." Alex felt a frustrated warmth creep up his neck.

Asha had a very reliable moral compass. Alex was used to exploring and pushing boundaries, safe in the knowledge that he could always count on his best friend's sense of true north. But they were growing up; the moral questions were becoming harder, the undergrowth denser and thornier. To be a good detective, Alex knew that he had to be able to navigate with his own set of tools.

He tried again. "I just think it's important to get inside Carlisle's head, even if it's kind of slimy in there. I'm not condoning blackmail, but the fact that Carlisle was able to threaten Dr. Ito probably means she did something wrong first. We need to understand all of their motives if we're going to understand any of them."

Asha didn't want to spend any more time in Carlisle's head than she had to, but she respected Alex's willingness to wade through the moral mud in search of the truth. "So, why did you ask to meet here at the park?"

Alex checked the time. "You'll see . . ."

The mischievous tilt to Alex's smile often made Asha feel like she was on the outside of a very clever inside joke. She hated that feeling. "Or you could tell me now," she said.

"Okay, okay." Alex brushed away a few acorns, shifting to a more strategic position under the tree. "The college that Carlisle applied to was in Dublin, Ireland. Would you like to know the name of this fine institution?"

"What?"

"Trinity College."

Asha looked across the street, leaning forward to see the top of the clock tower. "The Trinity Clock? That's a great lead!"

"I know. And guess what time it is . . ."

Asha looked at her phone. 4:58 p.m. *It's five o'clock somewhere.* They waited out the last two minutes in breathless silence. At five o'clock sharp, the Trinity Clock began to chime. It played the short, familiar melody that someone, somewhere must have decided was the appropriate tune for clocks. This was followed by five resonant clangs.

Nothing else happened.

A squirrel scurried up the trunk of the oak while a sparrow twittered on a low branch. Alex deflated. "I really thought I'd figured it out."

"It was a good guess." Asha tried to sound reassuring. She felt as though they had both taken a few wrong turns in a corn maze and were now having to retrace their steps to find another path. It was frustrating, but then, she reasoned, there was no use sitting at a dead end staring at a wall of corn. "Sometimes it's okay to backtrack."

Alex wasn't listening to her. His mind was already back on the limerick, turning over each line, searching for the secret that held it all together. He didn't even notice when a large, bluish drop of melted Popsicle trickled down his hand and landed on the red herring, staining it purple.

CHAPTER 6

THE CLOCK TOWER

Friday, July 7th

Asha was jerked out of sleep early the next morning by Alex, who was shaking her so hard that her teeth rattled.

"Asha! Asha, wake up!"

Asha groaned and sat up in bed, rubbing her eyes. "Alex? What are you doing here?"

"Your mom let me in."

"That doesn't really answer my question." Asha yawned. "What time is it?"

"It's six thirty. A perfectly reasonable hour."

If she had been more awake, Asha might have pointed out that Alex never replied to her messages before 10:00 a.m.

"Listen." Alex's hazel eyes were unusually green, as though lit from within by his unrestrained excitement. "I figured it out! I was so close yesterday—just missing one small piece. And now I've figured it out!"

"The limerick?" Asha made room on the bed so that Alex could sit down on top of her purple comforter.

Alex was almost too jittery to sit. "Do you know how many hours ahead Ireland is?"

"I don't know. Six?"

"Five," Alex corrected her. "So when it's five o'clock in Dublin, what time is it here?"

Fortunately for Asha, that math was easy enough, even for six in the morning. "Noon," she said.

Alex was so energized that he might as well have been levitating above the bedspread. "And what happens at the Trinity Clock at noon?"

Asha let out an audible gasp. "The automaton spectacle!"

"The automaton spectacle!" Alex sprang up in triumph.

The Trinity Clock, like a complex cuckoo clock, had several mechanical figures—some human, some animal—that marched out in front of the clockface every day at noon. The clockmaker had been famous for his automata in the 1800s. Alex liked to imagine an old man with magnifying goggles tinkering away with mechanical gears and levers.

The automaton spectacle might have seemed quaint and rather odd to an outsider, but to Asha and Alex it was just another part of life in Northbrook. Waverly College students would dress up the clockwork figures for Halloween and Christmas, but otherwise the daily spectacle was predictable and, therefore, forgettable. Alex's deduction, however, cast things in a whole new light.

There was no real possibility of her going back to sleep after that, but there were still five hours to kill before noon. She shooed Alex out of her bedroom so she could get dressed, and then they used up some of their time making pancakes. Alex smothered his pancakes in equal parts butter and maple syrup. Asha preferred to eat hers with blueberry jam.

Around 11:00 a.m. they rode their bikes back to Pendleton Park, where they spent several minutes trying to find the spot with the best view of the Trinity Clock face. It was a warm day, and, as it was nearing noon, very few people were out and about in the park. A young mother was watching her toddler splash about in the fountain. A teenage couple sat locking lips under the oak tree where the detectives had met just the previous afternoon. Both Alex and Asha found this extremely off-putting; they shifted so that the couple was hidden by summer foliage.

At noon precisely, the Trinity Clock started to chime, and the automaton spectacle began. Two doors opened on either side of the clockface. A series of figures paraded out on a thin track that was nearly invisible from the ground. First, six clockwork sheep bounded across the track, followed by a little shepherdess with blond braids. An upright soldier with a tall hat marched mechanically along his path. A ballerina passed by, pirouetting while balanced on one pointed toe. A clockwork king came out of one door, and a clockwork queen emerged from the other; they met in the middle and bowed to each other. A brilliant blue peacock spread his enormous tail, momentarily blocking the clock.

Alex and Asha watched the procession of figures, looking for anything out of the ordinary. Asha spotted it first. "There—look!"

A little wooden bed was moving along the track. Kneeling beside the bed was a small boy whose hands were usually pressed together in prayer. Now, however, a book was resting on his arms so that he appeared to be reading instead of praying.

"We need to go up there to get that book," said Alex.

"So we need to talk to Carlisle," replied Asha.

It was not a pleasant thought.

They hoped that Quentin Carlisle would be more willing to forgive them for breaking into his office and stealing evidence if they brought him a gift. Asha suggested a box of fancy cigars, which she thought someone like Carlisle would smoke in an old black-and-white movie. Alex thought Carlisle might prefer the still-bloody heart of a newborn child. Since Asha and Alex didn't know how to procure either of those things, they decided instead to visit Charleston's Chocolatiers, which was right around the corner.

Regrettably, the chocolates softened in the summer heat and got a bit squashed in Asha's backpack. By the time they reached Carlisle's office, their gift looked very sad indeed.

Quentin Carlisle examined the chocolatey mess. "What's this?" he asked Alex.

"A peace offering?"

"I don't think so, Inspector Clouseau. If anything, *that* is a declaration of war." Carlisle swept the box of chocolates into the trash bin by his desk. "By the way, pulling a fire alarm when there's no fire is a misdemeanor."

"You know what isn't a misdemeanor?" Alex said, going on the offensive. "Blackmail."

Carlisle did not look worried.

"Dr. Ito confirmed our theory about the check . . . right before she ripped up the proof." To avoid further blame, Alex clarified, "She already knew you were the one blackmailing her. That's what her clue from Dr. Fairfleet was about."

"Oh, I'm well aware," Carlisle said darkly. "Dear Prudence isn't very happy with me. She chewed my ear off the other day. If I didn't know what I know . . ." He paused. "Let's just say that we've reached an uncomfortable stand-off, Prudence and I."

"We can't help you with Dr. Ito," Asha cut in. "You made a bad choice and now you have to deal with the consequences. What we can do is help you with your clue. We solved it."

"No kidding?" Carlisle ran a hand through his dark hair, which sprang back into position. "I'll be honest—I thought Alistair was just having a laugh at my expense."

"The limerick was alluding to the Trinity Clock and the automaton spectacle," Asha explained. "We need to get up into the clock tower. Can you let us in?"

"I have the key, but aside from the occasional rebellious coed and the old man who comes to repair the clock, no one goes up there. Why do you need to see the automatons anyway?"

"Actually, the plural of automaton is automata," Asha said and immediately wished that she hadn't.

Carlisle stared at her coolly. "What's the plural for 'obnoxious pain in the neck'?"

"Are you going to help us or what?" Alex was still miffed that Carlisle had thrown perfectly good chocolate in the trash.

Asha was sure that Carlisle was going to say no, but instead he tossed the script he was reading onto the desk and swore. This seemed to be his way of agreeing to help. "I mean, what have I got to lose at this point?" he added by way of justification.

Carlisle led them to a small door in one corner of the lobby. There was a thick, old-fashioned iron lock, which Carlisle opened with a matching old-fashioned iron key. The door creaked open, revealing a dark shaft and a decaying ladder. The ladder, festooned with spiderwebs, disappeared into darkness before they could see where it ended.

"There you go," Carlisle said with a fake, grating sort of cheeriness. "Have a blast!"

"Aren't you coming with us?" Alex eyed the ladder apprehensively.

Carlisle leaned against the doorframe. "Tempting, but I think I'll pass. Thanks."

Asha and Alex stared up the shaft, each waiting for the other to make the first move. Asha was not especially scared of things one might find in a dark tower. Her fears were more abstract and grown up. For instance, she was afraid of Alzheimer's disease, which had killed her grandmother. And she was scared of letting Dr. Fairfleet down.

Alex was scared of many things that one might find in a tower: spiders, bats, rats, falling to his death. However, he was more afraid of looking like a coward in front of Asha. He made a lunge for the ladder and started to climb before his other fears could catch up with him.

Up they went, hand over hand. Alex broke most of the spiderwebs with his face, so Asha's climb was a lot less sticky and dusty. It was very dark, though, and every so often a rung on the old ladder would let out an unpleasant creak or crunch. At last they made it to the landing behind the enormous clockface. The room was dim, illuminated only by what little light seeped in around the circumference of the clock. The floor—if you could call it that—was nothing more than some boards placed strategically between the tracks for the automata.

And then there were the automata themselves. Up close, their paint was peeling, and the faces of the human figures appeared monstrous and threatening. There also seemed to be a lot more of them when they were packed into a small space than when they were on orderly parade in front of the clock. Alex and Asha were having a hard time finding the bed with the little boy.

After a few minutes, Alex spotted him. "Over here!" he called out from the far side of the tower. Asha made her way over to him, shuffling along the maze of boards and planks.

Because the wooden bed was bulky, it was isolated in its own corner, several feet away from the other figures. A narrow plank connected its track to the board where Alex and Asha were standing—a narrow plank suspended over a pit of foreboding darkness.

Alex tested the plank with his toe. "I've got this."

"Be careful!"

He stepped forward. "Gee, thanks for the advice. Because I was thinking about trying to cartwheel across—"

No sooner had Alex spoken than the great bell of the Trinity Clock rang out for one o'clock. The tolling of the clock could be heard from anywhere on campus. In the clock tower itself, the noise was deafening. Asha clapped her hands over her ears. Alex crouched, trying to steady himself as the plank vibrated under his feet.

When the echoing chimes finally died down, Asha lowered her hands. Alex allowed himself a little breath of relief and straightened up. And that was when the plank snapped. The broken board plummeted into the darkness below, and Alex dropped with it. He managed to grab onto the nearest bit of track, his legs dangling in space. The plank hit the ground somewhere far below with a clatter and a thud.

"Help!" Alex wheezed.

Asha let out a strangled squeak. She flopped down on her stomach to distribute her weight more evenly across the boards and reached out to grab Alex's arms.

Alex was both light and strong, but the physics of the situation were not in their favor. For a few agonizing seconds, Asha felt her partner's hand slipping out of her grasp. Then she gave a mighty tug, and Alex heaved himself up with his elbows. He rolled onto the board and lay there for a moment, breathing heavily and staring at the rafters.

When he had recovered his breath, Alex sat up next to Asha. They considered the plankless expanse between them and the clockwork boy by the bed.

"Now what?" Alex asked.

"Well," Asha ventured, "I think I can make it to the bed by walking on the track."

Alex looked at the track, which was about six inches wide with two raised metal ridges on either side, and then he looked at Asha, who was apparently crazy. "I'm sorry—did you miss the part where I almost fell and broke my neck?"

"I saw it," Asha snapped back. "I also saw our only other option disappear into the abyss."

Alex raised his eyebrows and took out his phone.

"What are you doing?"

"Getting ready to call 911."

Alex's doubt was all the prodding Asha needed. Like a gymnast on a balance beam, she put one foot in front of the other, holding her arms out to stabilize herself and refusing to look down. As soon as the bedpost was within reach, she leaned forward and clutched it. Only then did she realize that her heart was beating very fast.

Now that she was right next to the clockwork boy, Asha could see that he was holding a leather folder of some sort. She tugged it free and tossed it to Alex, who caught it with both hands. Then it was just a matter of making the return journey—one foot in front of the other—until she felt the solid, flat board under her feet, and she let her knees go weak.

Watching Asha's triumphant balancing act, Alex felt a combination of annoyance and total awe. He shook his head and muttered, "Unbelievable," which conveniently summed up both emotions.

"Let's go," Asha said, still shaking.

Since it was too dark to investigate the folder in the clock tower, Alex agreed to lead the descent. Climbing down the ladder seemed to take a lot less time than climbing up had. At the base of the tower, they found Quentin Carlisle standing in the doorway, looking irritated and—if such a thing were possible—a little bit concerned.

"I heard something fall on the other side of the wall. What happened?" demanded the director.

"Were you *worried* about us, Carlisle?" Alex adopted a tone of mock sincerity. "I'm touched."

"I'm worried about having to face two separate lawsuits and being known in the papers as the Clock Tower Child Killer."

"I think that's catchy, actually."

Their sparring was cut short when Asha took the leather folder out of Alex's hands and opened it. Alex pressed in close to get a better look. Even Carlisle seemed curious.

It appeared to be a sketchbook or portfolio of some sort. There were pages of charcoal and pencil drawings in various stages of completion. A sketch of a mother nursing her baby. A portrait of a wrinkled old man. A series of disembodied hands and eyes. As the sketches progressed, the drawings became more abstract and free form. Some of the sketches had little dabs of color next to them.

Asha flipped back through the portfolio to the first page, upon which the artist had recorded her name and the year:

Prudence Ito
1980

Alex snatched the sketchbook from Asha with keen interest. "This is Dr. Ito's artwork?"

They paused at a flawless charcoal study of the *Mona Lisa*. "I didn't know she could draw like that," Asha said.

"She's got a good eye for imitation, don't you think?" Quentin Carlisle's curiosity was fading. His face assumed its usual expression of superiority and boredom. "She went to art school but couldn't cut it. Dropped out in her second year. She enrolled at Harvard a few years later to get her doctorate in art history. A better fit, I suppose. You know what they say about those who can't do . . ."

Alex flared up in defense of Dr. Ito. "What? They direct community theater productions?"

"Hang on," Asha interrupted before Carlisle could deliver a scathing rebuke and derail the conversation further. "How do you know all that stuff about Dr. Ito?"

"Rumors circulate," Carlisle replied vaguely. "And I've seen most of those sketches before. I guess poor old Alistair isn't as many steps ahead as he thinks he is."

Leafing through the pages, Alex was so transfixed by Dr. Ito's work that he forgot to be angry with Carlisle. The theater director was right; Dr. Ito had a good eye for imitation. There were excellent studies of other famous paintings: *The Birth of Venus. Girl with a Pearl Earring. The Starry Night.* As Alex turned the last page, a piece of paper fell out of the folder and fluttered to the ground. It wasn't the same heavy, textured paper as the rest of the sketchbook. It was a piece of creamy Fairfleet stationery.

Asha bent down to pick it up and read aloud from the paper: "*'When we are born, we cry that we are come to this great stage of fools.' 25-17*"

"Ain't that the truth," Carlisle drawled.

"*King Lear?*" Asha asked.

"Act four, scene six," Carlisle replied. Asha had to hand it to him—the man knew his Shakespeare.

"What do these numbers mean?" Asha asked. "Twenty-five, seventeen? Dr. Ito's Shakespeare clue had the number five after it, but I thought it was referring to the act."

"More of Alistair's gibberish, I expect."

Alex shut the folder gently so as not to bend any of the pages. "We'll be taking this as evidence."

Carlisle checked his Rolex. "If it gets you two out of my hair, it's all yours. Like I said, I already know what's in that folder anyway."

"We'll get out of your hair for now," Alex said with a meaningful look at Carlisle's styled waves. "But we'll be back if we have any further questions."

"Cheers. When you call my assistant, tell her to set up our next meeting outside. Then you can bring Scooby-Doo, and maybe the gang will finally be able to close the case of the useless distraction."

Alex couldn't think of a comeback quickly enough. As the smirking director walked back to his office, Alex clutched the portfolio tightly to his chest. He hoped that Dr. Fairfleet had left them some truly incriminating evidence. Visions of Carlisle being fired, publicly humiliated, or taken into custody by the CIA played on a tantalizing loop in his imagination. Alex squared his shoulders and gritted his teeth. It was time to get to work.

CHAPTER 7

EXCESSIVE HEAT WARNING

Sunday, July 9th

When the weekend came, the weather turned hot. Too hot for walking downtown, and certainly too hot for amicable detective work. The sun glared down at Northbrook, causing the trees to droop and the tar on driveways to turn sticky. In the heat, Asha had less patience and Alex less restraint. It was a bad combination, made worse by the fact that they hadn't made any meaningful progress on the case in almost forty-eight hours. The countdown to July 15th felt like it was speeding up every day. They desperately needed a break—either in the weather or in the case, it didn't much matter which.

At noon, when the tree house was at its stuffiest, Alex and Asha met to go over the clues they had collected so far. Alex draped a semi-frozen towel over the oscillating fan so that it blew cold air throughout the tree house, a futile attempt to combat the rising temperature.

He lay on the floor in front of the fan, staring up at the sloped ceiling and the thick tree branch that served as a central beam. "What I don't get," he said, "is why we have a Shakespeare clue for each of the directors except Dr. Wright."

"We never finished the treasure hunt at the natural history museum," Asha reasoned. "There's still the clue about Athena, remember?"

Unable to get comfortable, Alex stretched his arms out over his head. "Do you have that picture of Dr. Fairfleet on you? Can I take a look?"

More annoyed than she should have been—because of course she had it on her, she always had all of their clues on her—Asha flipped to the page in her notebook where she had placed the photograph of a middle-aged Dr. Fairfleet at Eremos. She gave the picture to Alex, who held it in front of his face without sitting up.

"I bet Northbrook is about as hot as the desert right now," Alex grumbled.

But Asha wasn't listening to him; she was inspecting a faint blue smudge on the open piece of notebook paper.

"Alex," she said. "What would you say is the first rule of detective work?"

"Never trust the authorities."

"No, the other first rule."

"Don't run with a loaded weapon?"

Asha shook her head in mild exasperation. "It's a rule that's actually relevant to us. You say it all the time!"

Alex sat up. "You mean 'always check the back'? Hang on . . ." He glanced down at the photograph. "You can't be serious."

In one deliberate motion, he turned over the photo and set it on the floor. And there it was, bright and bold in Dr. Fairfleet's signature blue ink: another Shakespeare quotation.

"I am a man more sinned against than sinning." 19

Alex looked as though he had been slapped in the face with a piece of Mr. Behrman's red herring. "I can't *believe* we didn't check the back!"

"Now we have four Shakespeare clues—one for each director." Asha turned to a clean page in her notebook and wrote down the quotations so they could consider them all together.

Minnie: "Unhappy that I am, I cannot heave my heart into my mouth." W. S.

Dr. Ito: "Jesters do oft prove prophets." -5

Carlisle: "When we are born, we cry that we are come to this great stage of fools." 25-17

Dr. Wright: "I am a man more sinned against than sinning." 19

Alex studied the quotations. "Quentin Carlisle's clue sort of makes sense since it's about the theater," he said. "I don't understand any of the rest of them."

"Dr. Wright's clue makes him sound like a victim."

Alex made a noncommittal grunting noise that suggested he wasn't persuaded by this logic. "What about the numbers? It could be a code." He looked around for a pencil, invigorated by the prospect of some good old-fashioned code breaking.

Asha flicked through the pages of her notebook. "I think you're right. Minnie's clue says that we're supposed to 'put the pieces in order.' Dr. Fairfleet couldn't have known which clues we would solve first. What if we need to put the *quotations* in order and then work with the numbers?"

Alex agreed that it was a reasonable starting place. He looked up the quotations while Asha jotted down the act and scene for each in her notebook. They soon had a new order:

Minnie: "Unhappy that I am, I cannot heave my heart into my mouth." W. S.
(Act 1, Scene 1)

Dr. Wright: "I am a man more sinned against than sinning." 19
(Act 3, Scene 2)

Carlisle: "When we are born, we cry that we are come to this great stage of fools." 25-17
(Act 4, Scene 6)

Dr. Ito: "Jesters do oft prove prophets." -5
(Act 5, Scene 3)

"19, 25, 17, 5. Do those numbers mean anything to you?" Asha asked. "A combination to a lock?"

Alex nodded as he considered this possibility. "That's promising. But where's the lock?"

"No idea. Maybe we haven't found that clue yet."

"There are seven digits," Alex mused, "and some Northbrook phone numbers start with one nine two."

Asha took out her phone and dialed the number along with Northbrook's area code. It rang three times before a woman answered. "Daisy's Dry Cleaning. How can I help you?"

"Oh, hi!" Asha said, her voice unnaturally bright. She realized that they should have worked out what to say before she dialed the number. "I'm wondering if I can come pick up an order for Dr. Alistair Fairfleet?"

There was a pause on the other end of the line. "You mean the missing millionaire?"

"Umm, yes. That's the one."

"He's not a customer of ours." The woman's tone took on a suspicious edge. "Who is this? If this is another prank call, I'm calling the police."

Asha hung up.

"Smooth," said Alex. He couldn't quite help himself.

Asha bristled but kept her cool. "The lady on the phone sounded pretty defensive. It might be worth a visit in person." She snapped her notebook shut. "In fact, I think I'll go check it out."

Alex stared out the window at the limp leaves of the oak tree. "Now? It's a hundred degrees outside!"

"And we only have six days left," Asha reminded him. "You don't have to come."

But he did, of course. Alex wasn't about to let his partner stake out a local business all by herself. They rode their bikes into town and found a bench in the shade where they had a clear view of Daisy's Dry Cleaning and where it was only sweltering as opposed to scorching hot.

Asha took out a copy of *The Northbrook Nail* and pretended to read it, always keeping one eye on the target. Alex tapped out a repetitive drumbeat on the worn wood of the bench. The minutes inched by.

"How long do we have to sit here?" Alex asked. A bead of sweat trickled down the back of his neck. Stakeouts, as it turned out, were desperately boring. "What are we waiting for anyway?"

"We're looking for anything suspicious—anything that doesn't fit the scene." Asha didn't bother responding to his first question.

They waited and watched as three customers entered the cleaners. All three departed carrying clear plastic bags with unsuspicious shirts and dresses. Alex was just about to give up and leave when he spotted a potential suspect.

A young man had emerged from the alleyway beside Daisy's Dry Cleaning. The teenager wore ugly aviator sunglasses and a wrinkled, half-tucked polo shirt. In his gangly arms, he held a sleek white box.

Alex nudged Asha in the ribs, adding an unnecessary "*Psst.*"

Asha watched the youth over the top of her newspaper. He stopped to adjust his grip on the box and looked left and right before proceeding. He was being cautious, Asha observed. Maybe a little too cautious, Alex decided.

"We've got to follow him," Alex said.

"Why?" Asha put down her newspaper but didn't budge from her seat on the bench.

"What do you mean, *why*? Look at him. Look at his sunglasses."

"People wear sunglasses when it's sunny out," Asha noted tartly.

The teenager took out his car keys and got into a white van that was parked on the street. The engine came to life with a cough. Boxy, windowless, and unmarked, the van did not, in Alex's professional opinion, *fit the scene.*

"I'm going after him," Alex told Asha. He was done with this stakeout business. A chase was more his speed.

"You can't just leave when we're in the middle of surveillance!"

"Actually I can. You don't have to come."

But she did, of course. Asha wasn't about to let her partner chase an unmarked van all by himself. They grabbed their bikes from the curb and took off after the offending vehicle.

It was a much more evenly matched chase than it had any right to be. The van seemed to hit every red light on Main Street, spluttering to a halt and then lurching forward when the light turned green. Meanwhile Alex and Asha pedaled madly in the afternoon heat. Eventually, the van turned down a residential street, and they were able to make up some ground by cutting through the backyard of the McAllisters' Victorian bed-and-breakfast. After three more blocks, two sudden turns, and one close call with an unleashed Scottish terrier, they saw the van pull to a stop in front of a quaint brick house.

The detectives stashed their bikes in the bushes and dropped low beside them so they could watch the house without being seen themselves. Mr. Sunglasses, clutching the white box once more, made his way up the driveway and rang the doorbell.

It was a little girl, not much older than five, who answered the door. She was dressed as a ballerina, with a floppy pink tutu and a high, wispy bun. Her enormous brown eyes widened at the sight of the boy with the box.

"For me?" The little ballerina stood on her tiptoes and reached for the lid.

"STOP!" Without thinking, Alex leapt to his feet and launched himself through the bushes. The sunglass-clad courier was so startled that he dropped the box. It landed on the ground with a nonthreatening squelch.

"Are you kidding me?" The teenager rounded on Alex, his aviators reflecting Alex's stricken face. "What's your problem?"

Alex had no plan. The box seemed flimsier and much less dangerous than it had mere moments before. Asha joined him from the bushes, looking embarrassed on his behalf. Alex wished she would just let him clean up this mess on his own.

Mr. Sunglasses bent down to open the box, and they all stared at its contents. Twelve cupcakes decorated to look like Cookie Monster stared back. One of the cupcakes had been badly squashed. Its sugar-spun googly eyes were askew, and a half-moon of chocolate chip cookie had fallen out of its mouth, leaving a toothless gash in the frosting.

The little girl took one look at her cupcakes and began to bawl.

Asha cringed as the situation slid into focus. "Daisy's Dry Cleaning is right next to The Baker's Dozen."

"I figured that out for myself, thanks," Alex snapped. He knelt beside the sobbing child. "Please don't cry. Look!" He picked up the flattened Cookie Monster and tried to mash it back into shape. His efforts only made things worse. Alex's fingers came away blue, and a truly monstrous cookie creature screamed at him in silent anguish. The cupcake monster's eyes drooped sideways. The ballerina froze for a moment in horror. Then its eyes fell clean off, and she started wailing even louder than before.

Asha grabbed Alex by the arm and dragged him away from the scene of the crime. The little girl ran inside, shrieking for her mother.

"Are you happy now?" Asha asked.

"Of course not! What, do you think I'm some sort of . . ." Alex glanced back at the box of Cookie Monsters, his face pale.

"Now we've wasted half an afternoon," Asha said. It sounded like an accusation.

An indignant flush crept into Alex's cheeks. "You're the one who decided that a stakeout was a good idea. Daisy's Dry Cleaning is obviously a dead end!"

Asha was inclined to agree with Alex, but she wasn't prepared to tell him so. Instead, she busied herself extracting her bicycle from the bushes.

Alex gave Mr. Sunglasses a crumpled five-dollar bill for the squashed Cookie Monster. The detectives did not discuss their plans for the rest of the afternoon, but when they rode home, they took different routes. The heat was relentless. They both needed a chance to cool off.

Alex dedicated the next few hours to his latest digital art project. Asha curled up in her favorite armchair with a stack of well-worn books, familiar old friends. She could stand Alex for a lot longer than she could stand most people, but when she felt herself getting irritated with him, it usually meant she needed to take a break and spend a few hours with Harriet the Spy or Bilbo Baggins instead.

For a true detective, however, the call of an unsolved mystery cannot be ignored for long. Asha's mind kept wandering back to the Shakespeare quotations. Alex found that the creation on his computer screen was starting to look a lot like the intriguing temple carvings in the photograph of Eremos. By 7:00 p.m., they were both back in the tree house.

Alex had his laptop out and was working through several possible ciphers with the *King Lear* numbers. "Is 'aibeage' a word?" he asked.

"Cabbage?"

"No, aibeage."

"Not in English," Asha said. She was looking through Dr. Ito's sketchbook, searching for any additional clues that Dr. Fairfleet might have left them. She thought the more realistic drawings in the notebook were quite good, and she didn't understand why Dr. Ito's style changed so dramatically toward the end of the portfolio.

Asha paused on a page of charcoal swirls. Several dabs of paint—mostly blues and purples—were crowded in the leftmost margin. There was something familiar about the swirling pattern . . .

"Alex, do you recognize this?"

Alex plopped down next to her and examined the page. "I know those colors!" He pulled the sketchbook in close to his face and then slowly pushed it away as though playing with a Magic Eye book. "That's her, all right. The Gremlin de Tang!"

"*La Grenouille de l'étang?* Let me see!" Asha snatched back the sketchbook. Sure enough, she could now make out the face of a frog with a spiraling tongue amid the swirls.

The discovery of the frog prompted twenty minutes of frenzied research. Alex compared Dr. Ito's drawings to pictures of the famous painting online and discovered that there were at least four other sketches in the portfolio that seemed to be copying elements of *La Grenouille de l'étang*.

Asha found an entry about the painting on an art history website. "Listen to this." She began to read aloud: "'A masterpiece of the mysterious French artist known as Le Merle, *La Grenouille de l'étang* was a global phenomenon from its debut. The painting was initially housed in the Centre Pompidou in Paris, but it was auctioned off to private collectors when the museum reorganized its contemporary wing. Over the years the painting switched hands so many times that it could no longer be traced in public records. *La Grenouille de l'étang* was presumed lost until it was discovered in an estate sale by Dr. Prudence Ito of the Fairfleet Institute. The painting is now part of the permanent collection at the Fairfleet Museum of Art.'"

When she finished reading, Asha fell silent. Her face was grave. "Do you remember what Dr. Ito said about why it's important to have a clear record of ownership for a piece of art?"

Alex watched the calculation being performed behind Asha's dark eyes, and he arrived at the solution mere seconds after she did. "Asha, no. Just no."

"But it makes sense! Look at her sketches of *The Starry Night* and the *Mona Lisa*. We know she has a talent for imitation."

"There are plenty of reasons for an artist to sketch a famous painting that don't have anything to do with . . ." He trailed off.

"Forgery," Asha finished his sentence for him. Neither of them spoke. The silence in the tree house was suffocating.

Finally, Alex said, "Artists practice their craft by imitating famous works all the time."

"Do they get blackmailed for it?" Asha persisted. "Think about it, Alex. If Carlisle knew the most important piece of art in the Fairfleet collection was a fake, he could *easily* blackmail Dr. Ito for twenty thousand dollars."

Alex was becoming agitated. Even with a light evening breeze coming through the window, the tree house felt much too hot. "You can't forge a painting by a contemporary artist!"

"You can if the artist never takes credit for his work. Or if you're willing to take the risk that he's dead, which is what Dr. Ito thinks."

Alex was out of objections. If he had believed Asha was wrong, he might have been less upset. However, he thought she was probably right, and—by the strange paradox that is human nature—that made him hungry for a fight.

"Look," he said with the tense, trembling quality of a rubber band about to snap, "even if I were ready to admit that the painting is a forgery—which I'm *not*—what exactly do you want to do about it?"

Asha's face hardened, a shield against Alex's anger. "We need to tell someone."

"Oh yeah?" Alex shot back. "Like who? You can't tell the police without explaining everything about the case. And you can't tell Dr. Fairfleet because he's missing. Anyway, he obviously knows already."

Asha took a deep breath, aware of the effect that her next words would have. "Then I'll tell Dr. Wright."

"Dr. Wright?" Alex was truly stunned. "*Dr. Wright!* You're going to betray Dr. Ito to our number one suspect?"

"He's *not* our number one suspect. You just think that because you care about Minnie and now you like Dr. Ito too. Your personal bias is clouding your judgment. A good detective would never let that happen."

Alex clenched his hands. His toes curled in his sneakers. "It's called intuition, and it's a detective's most valuable tool. Maybe you'd understand if you weren't such a stuck-up killjoy."

Asha's boiling point was a lot higher than Alex's, but she had been simmering ever since the Cookie Monster incident. "At least I don't pretend to be a rebel when really I'm a pathetic lapdog to any authority figure who pats me on the head."

"You wanna say that to me one more time?" Alex seethed.

As it had been a rather complicated sentence to repeat word for word, Asha paraphrased. "You're a coward, Alex. Grow a moral backbone."

"And you're a snitch! Morality isn't always black and white!"

Asha closed her eyes and steadied herself before she said, "Fortunately, it only takes one of us to do the right thing."

Alex drew himself up to his full height. "Asha, if you go to Dr. Wright about the painting, that's it. We're over. You can consider the A&A Detective Agency dissolved."

Asha was caught off guard by the severity of Alex's threat. She opened her mouth to speak but then shut it again, worried that her voice would give her away. She didn't want Alex to know he had succeeded in wounding her.

"I think you should go," Alex said.

"This is our office."

"Yeah, but it's *my* tree house."

Asha stared at him for a moment. "Fine," she said, shoving her notebook into her backpack and slinging it over one shoulder. "Fine," she repeated. Asha climbed down the rope ladder, her grip so tight that every rung cut into her palms. She waited until she was safely out of Alex's yard and around the corner of the house to start crying. When she finally let them fall, her tears were silent and angry.

Back in the tree house, Alex collapsed into the hammock. He threw one of the pillows across the room as hard as he could. It collided with the bookshelf, causing two books to thud onto the floor. He was furious with Asha for being so inflexible and furious with Dr. Ito for forging the painting and, above all, furious with himself for letting his emotions get the best of him.

Swaying slowly, stewing in an unpleasant soup of guilt and anger, Alex remained in the hammock until the sun set behind the trees and he fell into an uneasy sleep. His dreams were scattered, but in all of them he was alone, and in all of them he wished he wasn't.

CHAPTER 8

A RARE AND VALUABLE THING

Monday, July 10th

The heat wave broke on Monday thanks to a massive thunderstorm that swept through Northbrook. Rain fell in thick sheets, and thunder rolled through the valley. Although it was the perfect sort of day to stay in bed with a good book, Asha—still reeling from her fight with Alex—couldn't settle in. She got a stomachache every time she thought of their argument.

Casting aside her copy of *A Wizard of Earthsea*, Asha pulled on her bright yellow raincoat and her rubber boots. She plunged into the storm, where she was met with a gust of wind that sneezed a cloud of cold raindrops right into her face. Asha knew she was headed for the Museum of Natural History, but that was about all she knew. She didn't know what she was going to say to Dr. Wright once she got there or whether Dr. Wright would be there at all; the Fairfleet museums were closed on Mondays. Asha thought that her risky journey into the storm was unlikely to pay off. Maybe she just wanted a good soaking to wash away her guilt.

Luck was on her side, however, for as she approached the museum, she saw a warm light coming from the window of Dr. Wright's office. Standing in the bushes, she tapped on the glass. The curator peered through the foggy, rain-spattered pane. When he saw Asha, he took a ring of keys from his desk drawer, gesturing for her to meet him at the front doors of the museum.

"Quite a morning to be out on patrol," Dr. Wright said as they walked back to his office. He took her raincoat and gave it a shake outside his door before hanging it on the coatrack. "And alone? Where, may I ask, is Mr. Foster?"

"I guess you could say that we had a professional disagreement," Asha replied, staring at her rain boots.

"I see," Dr. Wright said, and Asha suspected that he saw quite a lot.

"There's something I'd like to tell you, but I'm not sure if I should." She glanced up at the ceiling and then back down at her hands—anything to avoid Dr. Wright's gaze. "So maybe I won't just yet."

Asha expected that this response would bring out Dr. Wright's grumpy side, but instead he reached into his pocket and took out a small tin. "Ginger candy?"

He let Asha take a piece before popping one into his own mouth. The candy had a strong, spicy flavor that reminded Asha of her aunties' cooking.

"We can chat about something else, if you like. I hear you're quite the reader. What are you reading these days?"

This question never failed to energize Asha. "I'm on a bit of a fantasy kick right now, actually. I'm almost done with *A Wizard of Earthsea*. Next, I think I'm going to read *The Lord of the Rings*. I've read *The Hobbit* five times, and my dad says I'm ready for the real thing."

Dr. Wright turned a picture frame on his desk toward her. In the photo, Dr. Wright was standing next to a woman who must have been his wife and a tall, handsome boy. The woman and the boy both had beautiful smiles. Dr. Wright's smile looked forced—as though he had read about smiling but had never actually seen it done.

"This is my son, Joshua," he said. "He was an avid reader when he was your age too. Couldn't pry a book out of his hands if I tried. He's studying overseas now at

Oxford, my alma mater." There was a clear note of pride in Dr. Wright's voice.

Asha felt an unexpected warmth for Dr. Wright and decided to trust him with a question. "Can you help me with something?" She tore a page out of her notebook and wrote down the numbers from the *King Lear* clues—19, 25, 17, 5—before sliding the paper across the desk. "Do these numbers mean anything to you?"

Dr. Wright inspected the numbers with his trademark walrus frown. "I can't say that they do. A combination, maybe?"

"That was what we thought. The combination for a locker or a padlock somewhere?"

"Or a safe," Dr. Wright proposed.

This suggestion was so fitting and so thrilling that Asha decided it had to be true. "Minnie already knows the combination to the safe in the archives. Do you think there's another safe at Dr. Fairfleet's house?"

Dr. Wright sniffed. "Knowing Alistair, I imagine one would be hard-pressed to find a painting in his house *without* a safe behind it. That man would keep his dinner plates locked up with a code if the idea tickled him."

Asha did some quick thinking. She was certain that Dr. Fairfleet would never want her and Alex to break the law as part of their investigation, but it would be a different story if he wanted them to break into his own house. Then again, she wasn't confident that they had the skill set required to get into a millionaire's mansion in the first place. Unless . . .

Asha was struck by the memory of a fluffy black-and-white cat jumping onto her lap. Captain Nemo wanted to go home. And Minnie Mayflower had a key to Dr. Fairfleet's house.

Dr. Wright was watching her with interest. "You've had an epiphany."

"*Epiphany* is a little strong," Asha said. "Maybe just an idea. I need to talk to Alex." She wanted nothing more than to run to the tree house—rain or no rain—and tell her partner about her plan. Her insides did a horrible flip when she remembered that she had been exiled from the tree house and that Alex probably didn't want to talk to her at all.

Asha's distress must have shown on her face because Dr. Wright offered her another candy and said gently, "May I share some information with you? It's about my relationship with Alistair. You might find it illuminating."

"Sure." Asha took out a pencil and opened to a blank page in her notebook in case Dr. Wright said anything worth recording. "Go ahead."

"I've known Alistair for over thirty years now, and I like to think that he is my friend as well as my colleague.

However, I feel I would be remiss if I didn't tell you that we have had our fair share of—how did you put it?—*professional disagreements* over the years."

He paused to make sure Asha was paying close attention. "Near the beginning of my term as curator of the Museum of Natural History, we received a rare donation: an authentic Maya funeral mask. It was a stunning piece, made entirely of jade. Truly one of a kind. Unfortunately, the family making the donation couldn't account for the mask's provenance—do you know what that means?"

"The record of its origins and chain of ownership," Asha answered.

"Quite right. In the case of the Maya mask, some of the evidence seemed to point to looting. Guatemala wanted the mask back."

Asha put down her pencil to show she was listening.

"Alistair thought we should keep the mask. The provenance was hazy, after all. I believe he also felt that we could better care for the piece in our own museum. But in our line of work, we have a solemn responsibility to think about whose cultural heritage we are curating and how that heritage comes to us. My instincts told me that the mask had been stolen and, in the absence of clarity, that it ought to be returned to its homeland."

"If Dr. Fairfleet wasn't sure, why take the chance?" Asha asked. "Wouldn't a stolen artifact be bad for the museum's reputation?"

"That is my view of the matter. I wish I could say that these sorts of situations are rare, but sadly they are all too common. Museums all over the world curate artifacts of unclear provenance—or worse, artifacts whose unsavory histories are well known."

Museums all over the world. Asha considered the implications of this statement. One of her favorite memories was of a school trip to New York where she and Alex had first seen Egyptian mummies and tomb treasures. On a vacation with her parents in London, she had been fascinated to find sculptures and carvings from a temple in Rajasthan, India, not far from where her extended family lived. At the time, she had been curious to learn more about these exhibits and their origins, but she hadn't really thought about how the museums might have acquired them in the first place. Asha suddenly felt cold and clammy, and she didn't think her damp clothes were entirely to blame.

"What happened to the mask?" Asha asked, though she had a fair guess. She knew the museum's collection by heart, and she had never seen a mask made of jade.

"Alistair and I argued about it for weeks. Each of us knew that the other had a legitimate case, but neither of us was willing to cede any ground. Finally, I wrote a formal letter explaining my reasoning and asserting my privilege as executive curator of the museum. Then I sent the mask back to Guatemala."

Asha's eyes grew large; Dr. Wright's mail-in rebellion represented an ordinary act of courage, but an act of courage nonetheless. "Dr. Fairfleet must have been furious."

"I have never seen him so angry," Dr. Wright acknowledged. "It wasn't just the mask at stake. Alistair worried that I had set a dangerous precedent, jeopardizing our right to own and curate some of the Fairfleet Institute's most valuable artifacts."

"Like the Nabataean Zodiac?"

"No, not the Zodiac." Dr. Wright looked past Asha, as though he could see through the walls to the stone wheel in the Hall of Cultural Artifacts. "We know how the Nabataean Zodiac got here, and we can be proud of the story of its discovery."

Asha had a spark of insight and tried again. "The bust of Athena?"

This time Dr. Wright nodded. "Alistair moved the bust of Pallas Athena to the Museum of Art mere days after I returned the mask to Guatemala. I don't think he wanted to punish me, but he certainly meant to prevent the loss of another piece. So, you can understand why I don't think Alistair's riddle refers to 'giving up' the statue."

"That's not fair," Asha said.

"At that point, the bust of Athena was the least of my worries. I fully expected to lose my job."

"But you didn't."

"I did not. When the board of trustees found out what I had done, they wanted my head on a platter. Alistair defended me without a second thought. He understood why I had made my choice even if he disagreed with it, and he was able to convince the board that I had acted in the best interests of the museum. I've always been grateful for his support at that critical juncture."

Asha frowned down at her notebook. She wanted to be proud of Dr. Fairfleet for defending Dr. Wright, but she wasn't ready to overlook the fact that the bust of Athena was still sitting in the Museum of Art.

Dr. Wright seemed to sense her inner conflict. "Alistair is a flawed man, but he is also a good man—on occasion, even a great one. We do not always see eye to eye, but we respect one another because we both want what's best for this museum and the Institute. Do you understand what I'm trying to tell you?"

"I think you're saying that you don't have a motive for wanting Dr. Fairfleet gone."

"No." Dr. Wright shook his head impatiently. "I'm saying that you ought to cut Mr. Foster some slack. No matter how thickheaded he's been—and I've no doubt that Mr. Foster is capable of impressive thickheadedness—a good partnership is a rare and valuable thing in this world. Something worth preserving."

Outside, the rain was finally starting to let up. The steady rush of water at the window slowed to a trickle from the eaves. A gentle breeze blew the drops from the leaves of the trees, and a bird trilled somewhere in the museum gardens.

"Thank you, Dr. Wright," Asha said, and she meant it. "You've given me a lot to think about."

"Feel free to stop by any time, Miss Singh. You are most welcome here." And Asha could tell that he meant it too.

Earlier that morning, as Asha was putting on her raincoat and rubber boots, Alex was wondering if he had a raincoat at all. It didn't seem worth the trouble of trying to find one, so instead he snagged his mother's umbrella and set out on foot. The storm turned the umbrella inside out before he was halfway down the block. By the time he reached Minnie Mayflower's apartment above the Waverly College Library, he was thoroughly drenched.

Alex knocked, and Minnie opened the door, looking, as she often did, mildly astonished. "Alex, goodness! What are you doing out in this weather?"

She ushered him in. He stood dripping on the floral welcome mat. His curls sent rivulets of water down his face and the back of his neck.

"Wait here," Minnie said. She returned with a fleecy purple towel, which Alex used to dry his hair before draping it around his shoulders like a cape.

Minnie stared out into the curtains of rain. "Should I be expecting Asha this morning?"

"Not today," Alex replied. "We sort of had a fight."

"Oh dear." Minnie's cornflower blue eyes softened. "Do you want to talk about it?"

"Seeing as how it's possible the whole thing is my fault . . . no, I don't really want to talk about it."

"I'll make some tea then, shall I?"

Tea was not exactly Alex's cup of tea, but he was starting to feel uncomfortable in his wet clothes, and Minnie always added enough milk and sugar to make it drinkable. When she brought him a steaming mug, he mumbled his thanks and blew on the surface, sending mint-scented wisps out over the lip of the cup.

"Minnie," he said after a moment, "do you believe that good people can do bad things?"

"I suppose so," Minnie replied, as though this were a perfectly natural conversation starter. "But that question assumes there are good people and bad people in the first place. I tend to think there are just people and that most people are capable of good and bad actions." Minnie took a sip of her own tea. "Does this have something to do with the investigation?"

A part of Alex wanted to tell Minnie about Dr. Ito and the forged painting. Instead, he said, "There are too many suspects and too few suspects all at the same time."

Minnie murmured her agreement. "I can't imagine that any of the directors would want to harm Dr. Fairfleet. Not even Quentin Carlisle."

"Carlisle has motive," Alex said. "Dr. Fairfleet ruined his chances of getting a job at Trinity College Dublin after Carlisle forged his reference. Dr. Wright has motive because he wants to be chairman of the Institute. Dr. Ito has motive because"—he caught himself and changed course—"um . . . for the same reason as Dr. Wright. You're the only one without a motive, as far as I can tell. *You* don't want Dr. Fairfleet's job, do you?"

Minnie set down her teacup. "Alex, I can tell you with perfect candor that I would rather shovel manure for the zoo than take on Alistair Fairfleet's job. Sometimes I'm not even sure I want the job that I have." Surprised at her own words, Minnie turned pink with embarrassment. "Oh no. That makes me sound terribly ungrateful, doesn't it? And I truly am grateful. I owe so much to the Fairfleet Institute."

"Like what?" Alex asked.

"My education, to start. I was one of the first recipients of a Fairfleet Institute scholarship at Waverly College. And then there's this job." Minnie's blush deepened. She took another sip of tea to hide her face. "I'm sure you've heard by now that I wasn't the most qualified candidate for such a prestigious position. I almost didn't apply, but the timing . . ."

"The timing?" Alex prompted.

Minnie looked out the window at the rain. "My mother passed away last year. I took this job when she first got sick. Without it, I'm not sure what we would have done."

"Aw, Minnie. I didn't know that." Alex felt a pang of pity below his sternum. "I'm really sorry."

Minnie's eyes filled with tears so that they looked even more like pools of mountain spring water. "I miss her every day."

"What about your dad?"

"He died when I was a baby. He was never really in the picture anyway. It was always just me and my mother."

"So you're an orphan now?" The pangs intensified as Alex realized for the first time how lonely Minnie must be.

Minnie dabbed at the corner of her eyes with her cardigan. "I don't think they call you an orphan once you're an adult," she said, putting on a brave, if wobbly, smile.

Alex hoped that changing the subject would cheer Minnie up, or at least distract her. He felt terrible for making her so sad. "What would you do if you weren't principal archivist for the Institute?"

His diversion seemed to work; Minnie's face brightened considerably. "Oh, that's an easy one! I'd love to travel more." Minnie adjusted her skirt and sat up a little straighter in her armchair. "I've spent nearly all my life in Northbrook. I want to see the world. Paris, Buenos Aires, Edinburgh, Singapore . . ."

Alex let out a slow, silent breath, relieved that Minnie was no longer crying. "Yeah, Singapore sounds awesome."

Minnie was quiet for a moment, then shook her head as though clearing away daydreams of walking tours, restaurants, and museums. "But enough about me." She looked at Alex over the top of her gold-framed glasses. "If you want to get this investigation back on track, you need to patch things up with Asha. Were you in the wrong?"

Alex slumped back against the couch cushions. The woman sitting across from him was no longer suspect Minnie or victim Minnie; she was babysitter Minnie—the same Minnie who had once scolded him for deconstructing the vacuum cleaner to hunt ghosts.

"Asha's usually right about these sorts of things, so I guess I must be."

Minnie regarded him with gentle affection. "You don't always have to agree with your friends and loved ones, even about things that matter quite a lot. Sometimes the true value of a friend is having someone to talk to. I miss debating important questions with my mother almost as much as I miss laughing with her."

"Really?"

"Really. But that doesn't mean you can't apologize to Asha if the conversation didn't go the way you think it should have."

Alex nodded. The conversation certainly *hadn't* gone the way it should have. "What's the best way to apologize to a girl?"

Minnie pursed her lips in a small smile. "Girls are just people. How would you want someone to apologize to you?"

Alex thought about this. "I'd want them to get me ice cream. Or maybe pizza." He tilted his head, deep in concentration. "No, definitely ice cream."

"An ice-cream apology would be hard to turn down," Minnie agreed.

At the thought of working things out with Asha over ice cream, the little knot of anxiety that had been sitting in Alex's chest relaxed and began to untangle itself. He gave Minnie a grateful glance and gulped down the rest of his peppermint tea.

☙

The next day, Asha and Alex met up at The Sweet Spot, Northbrook's premier old-fashioned ice-cream parlor. They bought each other ice cream and sat down at a small table in the corner next to a ceramic statue of a grinning cow.

Asha bought Alex his favorite: triple chocolate ice cream with hot fudge, Oreo crumbles, and Reese's Pieces. Alex bought Asha her favorite: coconut ice cream with caramel sauce. In terms of money spent, Alex got the better end of the deal, but they both felt it was the symbolic nature of the gesture that mattered most.

They sat poking at their ice cream for a few awkward seconds before Alex broke into a hurried apology. "Look, Asha. I'm really sorry about the other day. You were right about the painting. We're the good guys—we can't lie or cover up a crime." He swirled the hot fudge around in his cup and said, "And I'm sorry I called you a stuck-up killjoy."

With this initial bridge crossed, Asha jumped at the chance to offer her own apology. "I'm sorry too. A good detective trusts their instincts and doesn't blindly accept authority." She thought about Dr. Wright risking his job to send the Maya mask back to Guatemala. "Sometimes the rules are wrong. And I'm sorry I called you a pathetic lapdog."

"Yeah, that one stung," Alex admitted.

Asha took a bite of her ice cream. The caramel was thick and syrupy-sweet. She had to fight past the gluey texture to continue the conversation. "I was thinking that maybe we could tell both Dr. Wright and Minnie about the painting. That way, even if one of them is a criminal, the other one will know the truth. And also," she added, in the spirit of compromise, "maybe you would want to talk to Dr. Ito first to hear her side of the story. Or at least to give her a heads-up that she's about to be exposed."

"Deal!" Alex waved his spoon in her direction for emphasis, accidentally flicking a drop of hot fudge onto her cheek.

They spent the next half hour finishing their ice cream and catching each other up on the previous day's interviews. When Alex recounted the death of Minnie's mother, Asha's throat tightened with a surge of sympathy. The undercurrent of sadness beneath the archivist's cheerful, glimmering surface suddenly made a lot more sense. Asha, in turn, told Alex about the Maya mask and the bust of Athena. Unlike Dr. Wright, Alex felt that this information strengthened the connection between the statue and the final scavenger hunt clue, though he wasn't sure how.

"Do you think the bust of Athena belongs in Greece?" Alex asked.

"I think that you can't just take things from other cultures and call it archaeology," Asha replied. "What about you?"

"I don't know," Alex said, and it felt good to admit as much to Asha. "My favorite thing about museums is that they let you see art and artifacts from all over the world. They're like portals for sharing culture and history. But I guess if you have to move or hide a piece of art to keep it, that's not the sort of sharing I'm talking about."

Asha listened thoughtfully as he spoke. "I think you're probably right about that," she agreed. She received a chocolate-smudged smile from Alex in return.

When there were no more details to divulge and the bottoms of their ice-cream cups had been scraped clean, Asha took out her notebook. She folded her hands in front of her, all business. "Now that the agency is fully operational again," she said with a devious glint in her eye that made Alex proud, "let me explain how we're going to break into Dr. Fairfleet's mansion."

CHAPTER 9

HOW TO BREAK INTO
THE FAIRFLEET MANSION

Tuesday, July 11th

STEP 1: MISDIRECT

"Now remember," Asha said as they marched up the back staircase to Minnie's apartment, "don't oversell it."

"Roger that. Urgent, but not *too* urgent." Alex put on a pained grimace and rapped on the door. When Minnie answered, he let out a long, loud groan before she could greet them. "*Aarrggh.* Minnie, I need to use your bathroom. I have the worst—*oorghf*—stomachache," he grunted.

Asha swallowed a sigh and kept her face blank. Alex was overselling it. Thankfully, Minnie was the sort of sweet soul who was willing to buy anyway.

"Good heavens!" Minnie blinked in alarm. "Of course—the bathroom is down the hall and to the left." Alex was already half sprinting, half waddling in the direction she had indicated. Minnie yelled after him, "Should I call your parents?"

"No!" Alex shouted back. "That's really not necessary. But I wouldn't say no to some Pepto-Bismol or—*errrggh.*"

Minnie ushered Asha in. "Hello, Asha dear. So glad that you two patched things up. If you'll just wait here while I see if I can find something for Alex . . ."

"Don't worry about me," Asha said, wiping her shoes on the welcome mat. Minnie gave her a distracted smile and hurried down the hall.

It took Asha longer than she would have liked to locate Captain Nemo, who had hidden under Minnie's favorite armchair to avoid the commotion. Asha was able to coax him out with gentle smooching noises and the promise of a catnip mouse toy. He wound himself around her ankles, as sinuous as a snake but much fluffier.

"I'm really sorry about this, Captain Nemo," Asha said, picking him up by his middle as he tried to squirm away.

"It's for the greater good." She set the black-and-white cat down in the coat closet and shut him inside. Then she made sure the exterior door was ajar before the archivist returned holding a bottle of pink medicine.

When Minnie saw the open door, she looked around frantically for the cat. "Oh! Oh no . . . Asha, have you seen Captain Nemo? Did he run outside?"

Asha remained tactfully silent.

Minnie ran to the back landing and peered over the railing. "I don't see him!" she moaned. "Here, kitty! Captain Nemo!"

Captain Nemo chose this moment to let out a disgruntled *mrowl* from the coat closet, but his soft complaint was drowned out by an explosive, trumpeting fart noise from the bathroom. Alex had just blown a very wet raspberry into his elbow.

Minnie's anxious gaze darted back and forth between the bathroom and the outside world. "I'm sure he's trying to get back home again. I can go pick him up from Dr. Fairfleet's, but I can't leave Alex here in his condition."

Right on cue, Alex emerged from the bathroom, his face flushed and slightly sweaty. In reality, he had spent the past few minutes splashing his face with hot water, but the effect was convincing. Despite herself, Asha was impressed.

"Minnie, will you take me home, please?"

Minnie looked so worried that Alex and Asha were struck by a shared twinge of guilt. "Of course," Minnie said. "We'll take my car. I'll drop both of you off on my way to look for Captain Nemo."

"Can I come with you?" Asha asked. "I want to help, and I think Alex might prefer to be alone for a while."

Alex made a sad, gurgling noise in agreement.

"Yes, all right. Come on then."

Minnie helped Alex to her car. Asha was the last one to leave. As she passed the coat closet, she surreptitiously turned the handle and left the door open a crack so that Captain Nemo would be able to escape. She dropped the little toy mouse on the ground for him. He had played his part and deserved his reward.

STEP 2: SCOUT

After a brief chat with Alex's mother, who thanked Minnie profusely for bringing him home, Minnie and Asha drove to the Fairfleet Mansion. It was a tasteful residence for such a grand estate. There were lots of large windows and a stately slate roof. Ivy climbed the old stone walls. The grounds, with rosebushes still in bloom, had all the romantic charm of an English garden.

Minnie's key let them in through a kitchen door near Captain Nemo's cat flap. Asha pretended to check her phone, but in fact she was watching as the archivist disabled the alarm system with a code: 1652. That was easy enough to remember; it was the year Northbrook had been founded.

Once inside, Asha followed Minnie through the halls as the archivist called for Captain Nemo. Asha couldn't do any real snooping, but she was able to get a general sense of the mansion's layout. She also had the opportunity to slip away from Minnie just long enough to unlock an inconspicuous side door.

Eventually, when Captain Nemo didn't respond to her calls, Minnie's shoulders sagged, and her expression sank. "I don't think he's here. He could be anywhere."

"He's probably back at your apartment," Asha reassured her, wondering if this technical truth could be considered a lie. "We didn't really look for him very hard before we left."

Minnie's brow creased, and Asha stopped talking. Minnie was sweet, but she wasn't stupid. Better to quit while she was ahead. Before they left, Minnie re-alarmed the security system and locked the kitchen door, but none of that mattered. Asha had an unlocked side door and the security code. All she needed now was Alex.

STEP 3: INFILTRATE

Despite Alex's protests that he was really, truly feeling better, he wasn't allowed out of the house that evening. Asha woke up early Wednesday morning while the grass was still wet with dew to collect Alex for their mission.

Thanks to the first two steps of the plan, the break-in itself was anticlimactic. They let themselves in through the side door, and Asha hurried to enter the code and disable the alarm. The house was still and silent.

"We should split up," Alex said without much conviction. "We'll cover more ground that way."

They didn't split up.

Asha and Alex roamed the many rooms of the mansion, tugging at picture frames and running their fingers over the walls to look for secret panels. All of the rooms were elegantly furnished, but most of them had an empty, stale quality. The fireplaces were free of soot and ash. The couches were plump and undimpled, as though they had never really been sat on. Only the kitchen and the master bedroom showed signs of habitation: a couple of plates in the drying rack, a dog-eared book on the bedside table, a faint whiff of Dr. Fairfleet's cedar aftershave in the bathroom.

Asha stopped to look at a collection of photographs on Dr. Fairfleet's bureau. They had seen several oil portraits during their search, but those paintings seemed formal and distant. These photographs, chosen by Dr. Fairfleet for comfort and company, were more personal.

"Alex, come look at these!"

There was a sepia-toned photograph of a couple on their wedding day. The man was wearing a World War II naval officer's uniform and looked enough like a young Dr. Fairfleet that Asha felt confident the couple must be his parents. In a much more recent photograph, Dr. Fairfleet sat on a park bench holding the hand of a tiny, frail old woman. Asha searched the face of the old woman on the bench and the young woman in her wedding dress, wondering if they were the same person.

Alex pointed to a framed oval portrait of a severe-looking matron wearing a high-necked dress and a dramatic hat from the turn of the twentieth century. "I bet that's Maude Fairfleet!" he said. He thought that the straight-backed woman in the picture would approve of Dr. Prudence Ito at the helm of her museum. They both seemed like women who could get the job done. Alex's smile dropped when he remembered that Maude Fairfleet probably *wouldn't* approve of the forged painting in the modern art wing.

Alex and Asha continued to examine the pictures on the bureau, pointing out funny details and speculating about the people in them. The final photograph was of Dr. Fairfleet and the other Institute directors. Dr. Wright and Dr. Ito were on his left, and Minnie and Carlisle were on his right. He was shaking hands with a beaming Minnie, who looked very pretty with her strawberry blond hair in a French twist.

"I guess the Institute really is like family to Dr. Fairfleet," Asha mused. She dusted off the frame before they left the room to continue their search.

After nearly an hour of fruitless investigation, Alex paused to ask a question that had been on his mind for a while. "Don't you think it's strange that Dr. Fairfleet doesn't have a workspace at his house? Like an office or something?"

Asha agreed that it was odd. Where were Dr. Fairfleet's personal files and papers? And surely he had a computer—Dr. Fairfleet was old, but he wasn't *that* old. "Maybe we missed it," she said. She had lost track of the number of rooms in the mansion.

"Or maybe it's hidden!"

"I'm not sure where you could hide a—" But she didn't finish her sentence. She was thinking of the library—a handsome room lined with floor-to-ceiling shelves. Something about the library had itched at her, and it occurred to her now that the room was smaller than it should have been if it really extended out to the eastern wall of the mansion. "The library . . ."

As though reading her thoughts, Alex clapped his hands together. "There's a secret bookshelf door, isn't there? *Please* tell me there's a secret bookshelf door!" He could barely contain his glee.

"There *might* be a secret bookshelf door," Asha said.

They sprinted to the library, where they were faced with shelf after shelf of leather-bound tomes. "Where do we start?" Asha asked. There were hundreds—possibly thousands—of books.

"What does Dr. Fairfleet like to read?"

They tried Shakespeare first. There was a copy of *King Lear* and a heavy *Complete Works*, but both came off the shelf with no noticeable effect. Next, they looked for books with words like "secret" or "key" in the title. Again, no luck.

Asha found an entire shelf of detective fiction. It featured many of the books that Dr. Fairfleet had asked them to read when they were starting the agency. She tried *The*

Maltese Falcon and *Death on the Nile*. After her conversation with Dr. Wright, Asha found that she was a little more skeptical of Dr. Fairfleet's reading recommendations—a little less inclined to excuse the flimsy femme fatales of the noir narratives or the British bias of the Golden Age classics. She tugged on the spine of *The Complete Father Brown Stories* with less reverence than she might once have afforded the crime-solving priest.

In any case, the detective fiction shelf was on the same wall as a window facing the front gardens. There was nowhere for a secret door to lead.

"There aren't any Sherlock Holmes books here," Alex observed. "What was the one we read last summer for Dr. Fairfleet?"

"*A Study in Scarlet.*"

Alex spent a few minutes searching the spines of the books on the most promising wall and grinned when he found a small cluster of Sherlock Holmes books at about eye level. "*A Study in Scarlet!* I've got it here!"

Asha put down the poetry collection she was holding and skipped over to watch as Alex tilted the spine. The book resisted this movement. Alex's grin widened, and he pulled harder. A hidden mechanism somewhere behind the book released with a click. A section of the shelf swung smoothly inward on well-oiled, invisible hinges.

The first thing they noticed as they peered into the secret room was the color. The plush carpet and drapes were a deep, rich red. The chair behind the mahogany desk had a red velvet seat cushion too.

"Ha," Alex chuckled. "A study in scarlet. Get it?"

Asha got it.

"Look for anywhere you could hide a small safe," Asha instructed. She was already inspecting a much smaller bookcase within the study. A secret bookshelf compartment within a secret bookshelf room would be right up Dr. Fairfleet's alley.

Alex started with the imposing desk. The drawers were locked, and the surface was tidy and organized. He riffled through a few stacks of boring, grown-up papers and uncapped one of Dr. Fairfleet's finest fountain pens before a small notepad near the corner of the desk caught his eye. On the top piece of paper were three animal pictographs drawn by a steady hand in deep blue ink:

"Blue ink. Weird symbols. I think this is for us." He peeled the sheet from the pad and handed it to Asha, who examined the symbols with interest.

As Asha stuck the slip of paper into her notebook, Alex turned his attention to one of the filing cabinets and then to a large antique globe on a stand in the corner.

"Be careful with that," Asha warned. "It's probably really expensive."

"I'm always careful!" Alex claimed, but as soon as her back was turned, he pulled a face and gave the globe a rebellious spin. One half of the orb came free and fell to the ground with a thud that was muffled by the carpet. In the remaining half of the globe, there was a sleek chrome safe.

Asha gave Alex a look of mixed exasperation and anticipation. "Go on, then. Try the combination," she prompted. "19-25-17-5."

Alex reached for the dial but stopped short. "We have a problem."

"What's wrong?"

"There aren't any numbers on this lock."

Asha stood on her tiptoes to get a better look over Alex's shoulder. Sure enough, there were no numbers. The lock featured a familiar sort of dial with a minimalist design. There was a single arrow on the turning mechanism as a marker. At fixed intervals around the outside of the dial, twelve lines had been etched into the chrome.

Asha counted the notches under her breath. "Twelve," she noted. "Maybe it's like a clock?"

"How many clock clues is Dr. Fairfleet going to give us?" Alex grumbled. He gave the dial an experimental twist. The motion was smooth and seamless, with just enough resistance to be satisfying.

"Wait, there's something else," Asha said. At the bottom of the safe underneath the lock was a small, engraved image. "It's an animal of some sort. A horse, maybe?"

"I think it's a camel." Alex had an idea. "Can I see that piece of paper I gave you earlier? The one with the other animal signs?"

Asha scrambled for her notebook and flipped through the pages until she found the paper that Alex had discovered on the desk.

Alex snatched the note from her. "Look—a fish, twin birds, and a ram. Pisces, Gemini, and Aries. There are twelve signs of the zodiac and twelve notches on the safe. And this engraving could represent the camel chest! It's like a mini version of the Nabataean Zodiac!"

"So if we know where the Zodiac signs belong, then the fish, the birds, and the ram tell us where to point the arrow." Asha nodded, catching on. "Dr. Fairfleet left the combination sitting out on his desk?"

"He left it sitting on his desk *for us*." Alex held the note up next to the dial. "We just need to remember where the animal statues were placed around the wheel in the Museum of Natural History . . . Do you remember where the animals were placed around the wheel?"

"No," Asha admitted.

"You didn't write it down in your notebook?"

"I didn't know we would need it!"

"This is the problem with your low-tech strategy," Alex said with a maddening sense of superiority. "You have to be selective. With the internet, on the other hand, I have the entire sum of human knowledge at my fingertips." Alex took out his phone and began to type. He frowned, held his phone up to the ceiling, and frowned harder. "Huh."

"You were saying?" Asha crossed her arms.

"No signal," Alex mumbled.

"Right." Asha turned to a blank page in her notebook and drew a circle with twelve lines. "We can try to recreate the Zodiac. I know the fish sculpture was here." She wrote "Pisces" at the appropriate point on the circle. "That's a third of the combination already."

Alex pointed at a line near the bottom of the circle. "The lion was there. And there was a crab right next to it."

"Good," Asha said. "The crab is Cancer—that's right after Gemini, I think, so the birds must go here on the other side." She penciled them all in.

Alex looked pleased with himself. "This isn't so hard!"

STEP 4: ESCAPE

The moment that this bold claim had passed his lips, there was an unexpected noise from somewhere in the house. A door creaked open and clicked closed. The young detectives froze.

There were footsteps—slow and uncertain ones, far away but drawing nearer.

Asha inched forward and shut the secret bookshelf door, closing them inside the scarlet study. They remained very still, listening to their own loud heartbeats and the occasional sound of muffled footsteps.

"Who do you think is out there?" Alex whispered. "Would Minnie come back?"

"It could be anyone. We need to get out of here," Asha replied. "Do you remember where the ram was on the wheel?"

"I remember a ram, a goat, and a bull, but I don't remember where any of them are supposed to go. Too many animals with horns."

There was a rustling noise on the other side of the bookshelf door. Whoever was in the house was now in the library. Asha's pulse sped up. Did the intruder suspect there was a secret room? If so, it was only a matter of time until they found the right book.

Alex made up his mind. "If it's just the ram that we're missing, I'm going to start trying possible combinations. Open the window and get ready to run." He nudged Asha out of the way and began fiddling with the dial.

Asha assessed the window—an old-fashioned, lead-paned rectangle that stretched from floor to ceiling. A small section near the top opened outward like an envelope flap. She released the latch, pushed open the window, and eyed the gap. It was going to be a tight squeeze.

"Any luck?" she asked.

"Not yet." Alex tried to block out everything except the safe and the lock. He nearly jumped out of his sneakers when a cell phone rang beyond the bookshelf barrier. Asha recognized the tune as the famous aria from Mozart's *The Magic Flute*. Despite her jangling nerves, she had to wonder what kind of person would use an opera aria for a ringtone. Alex wondered what kind of person would use a ringtone at all in this day and age.

"We can come back for the safe another day. We need to *go*," Asha hissed.

"Twenty more seconds," Alex said. "There aren't many combinations left."

"Alex—"

The mechanism of the door in the bookshelf caught with a *thunk* at the exact same moment that the lock of the safe clicked open. Inside the safe was a single cream-colored envelope.

Alex grabbed the envelope and tossed it to Asha, who crammed it into her backpack and reached for the high window ledge. Alex gave her a boost. Pushing her backpack out ahead of her, she shimmied through the gap. It was, as she had predicted, a tight fit, but if anyone could slip out of a window with grace, it was Asha. She landed softly in the flower bed below.

Alex's exit was somewhat less graceful. He heaved himself over the lip of the window, grunting as the lead pane pressed into his stomach. His sneakers squeaked against the glass, and the window frame gave a threatening groan as he shifted his weight and tipped headfirst into a blooming shrub next to Asha.

Pulling petals out of her hair, Asha was about to take off running when Alex grabbed her by the ankle and she fell right back down.

"Asha!" Alex's voice was strangled. "My shoe!"

"What?"

"*My shoe!*" Alex pointed at the window. One of his sneakers had gotten caught on the hardware and was now dangling by its laces.

"Leave it," Asha said sharply.

"But . . . it's my shoe!"

"You have other shoes!"

A shadow passed over the window. The intruder was in the study.

"Run!" Asha screeched.

And they ran. Or rather, Asha ran. With just one sneaker, Alex hobbled along at breakneck speed like an injured but very motivated chicken.

STEP 5: DEBRIEF

Back at the tree house, Alex and Asha were impatient to open the envelope they had taken from Dr. Fairfleet's safe. Asha removed the creamy piece of stationery from her bag and attempted to smooth it out on the floor, as it had gotten bent in their frantic escape.

On the front of the envelope, a date was printed in deep blue ink:

July 15th

"The fifteenth of July," Asha said. The date filled her with a dull sense of dread.

Alex's insides twisted. "That's only four days away. What do you think will happen to Dr. Fairfleet if we don't find him in time?"

"I don't know." Asha didn't want to know. "What do you think will happen if we find him too soon?"

"That doesn't seem likely at this point, does it?"

Asha didn't respond. She tore open the envelope more violently than she meant to. A single feather, large and glossy, floated to the ground. The feather was a steely shade of blue gray. It almost looked like a dagger, sharp-edged against the floorboards.

Picking up the feather and twirling it between his fingers, Alex asked, "Does it mean anything to you?"

"It's a feather." Asha couldn't keep the bitterness out of her voice. "Add it to the list of things we don't understand about this case." She took the feather from Alex and held it up in the beam of dusty light streaming from the window. It yielded no secrets.

Alex had nabbed a bag of marshmallows from the kitchen. He speared one with a fork and started roasting it over the flame of a small candle.

"We should have waited just a *second* longer to see the intruder," he lamented. His marshmallow caught fire, but instead of blowing it out, he watched the outer skin flare up and char.

"Too risky." Asha shook her head. "No one knew we were at the mansion. If the intruder was the person behind Dr. Fairfleet's disappearance, it would have been dangerous to stay."

"I guess that's true. This way we live to sleuth another day."

"And we're back to square one with the *King Lear* code. We're going to need all the days we can get."

Alex held out the blackened marshmallow for her. "Sometimes there's a tough break right before a big break." He sounded a lot more optimistic than Asha felt.

Asha placed the blue-gray feather between two blank pages of her notebook before she plucked the marshmallow from the end of the fork. The burnt sugar did little to cover up the taste of frustration that lingered in her mouth.

CHAPTER 10

THE EXCAVATION
OF XAVIER FAIRFLEET

Thursday, July 13th

July 15th crept ever closer—a line of fire just beyond the horizon—and the choking smoke that preceded it was the very real fear that they might fail. Asha and Alex resolved to dedicate all of their waking hours to solving the case. Even when they were sleeping, they often dreamed of Shakespeare and French frogs.

The *King Lear* code was still their most promising lead. Feeling that they had lost sight of the original context of the puzzle, the detectives decided to return to Minnie's apartment, where they had discovered the first Shakespeare quotation. Asha wanted to get back to the root of the clues—to think about the unfortunate king of Britain and his daughters. If nothing else, there were bound to be snacks at Minnie's place. They had exhausted nearly all of the supplies in the tree house.

Minnie had work to do for the archives, but she didn't seem to mind having Alex and Asha around as she pored over her paperwork. She even let them spread their various clues and scraps of Fairfleet stationery out over her coffee table. Asha sat cross-legged on the floor with her notebook in front of her and Captain Nemo in her lap. Alex flopped down on the couch, letting one arm drape over the edge. He thought he probably looked like Sherlock Holmes, relaxed and cerebral. Asha thought he looked like a fainting Victorian lady, or maybe a sick sloth.

"It's got to be a cipher," Alex repeated for the tenth time that morning. He was really stuck on ciphers. "We must be missing some sort of key. Or maybe there are more numbers. Remind me which numbers go with which clues?"

Asha patiently read the quotations to him:

"'Dr. Wright: *I am a man more sinned against than sinning.* 19. Carlisle: *When we are born, we cry that we are come to this great stage of fools.* 25-17. Dr. Ito: *Jesters do oft prove prophets.* -5.'"

Alex let his arm fall over his eyes so that he could think better.

Asha refocused her attention on the details. "There are dashes between 25 and 17 in Carlisle's clue and before the number 5 in Dr. Ito's clue, but there are no dashes before or after 19 in Dr. Wright's clue. What if 19 and 25 are supposed to go together? It could be a date: 1925." This idea glimmered with potential for Asha, though she couldn't yet pinpoint why.

"What about Minnie's clue?" Alex asked.

"Her clue isn't part of the code."

Alex sat up straight on the couch, forgetting all about his Sherlock Holmes pose. "That's weird, right? Are you sure?"

"Positive," Asha replied. "There's just the quotation and then William Shakespeare's initials . . ." Asha's breath caught in her throat. "Alex, you're a genius!"

"Of course I am." Alex flopped back against the couch cushions and met Asha's eye uncertainly. "Why? What'd I say?"

Asha shuffled the papers on the coffee table until she found Minnie's clue. "Read the postscript!" She passed the slip of stationery to Alex with an enthusiastic flourish.

"*Put the clues in order, but don't forget your initial observations.*'" Comprehension dawned on Alex's face, a subtle sunrise. "Your *initial* observations! Minnie's clue is followed by Shakespeare's initials—W. S.!"

In a moment of earnest if somewhat unprofessional excitement, Alex and Asha exchanged a single high five.

"Can I have a piece of paper?" Alex asked.

Asha tore one out of her notebook and watched as he began making frantic notes in his messy handwriting.

"If it's a code," Alex mumbled, "it could be a clue to shift the cipher. W to S. If we take a standard cipher where a = 1 and move all the letters back four places, we end up with . . ." He scribbled the solution down on the paper and held it triumphantly aloft to read it aloud. "'Wexawca.'" Alex's face fell. "Well, that's even worse than 'aibeage.'"

At that moment, Minnie entered the living room, carrying a bowl of microwave popcorn to offer as a snack. "You two seem excited," she observed.

"We've made a breakthrough," Asha told her.

"Though where we've broken through to remains to be seen," Alex said.

"We think the initials W. S. are meant to help us figure out the *King Lear* code. Look." Making sure that the dashes were in their proper places this time, Asha held out the full code for her to see: W. S. 19 25-17-5.

Minnie looked. And then she let out a hiccup of surprise. Making a sudden gesture with her hands, the archivist dropped the bowl of popcorn. Kernels flew up into the air and fell to the floor like fluffy snowflakes.

Minnie took the code from Asha and stared at it hard. "It's an archival number! The W. S. doesn't stand for William Shakespeare, it stands for—"

"Wadsworth Stacks," Asha and Minnie said at the same time.

"How could I have missed that?" Minnie pressed a hand to her forehead. "The first numbers indicate the year—in this case 1925—then it tells me the box number and the file number."

Asha felt a fluttering in her stomach that was much more like a flock of seagulls than a swarm of butterflies. "Minnie, can we go to the archives to find whatever it is that the number is for?" She rocked on the balls of her feet. "Now?" she added, too excited to be polite.

Minnie didn't need to be strong-armed. "Yes—oh, of course!" the archivist said breathlessly, and she took off down the hall toward the archives, the detectives trailing close behind.

The archives were dim and cool, drawing Asha and Alex into their strange any-time-of-day twilight. Minnie knew exactly where the 1925 archives were housed, but she had to turn one of the large crank handles to separate the rarely accessed shelves. She consulted the slip of paper Asha had given her, muttering to herself: "Box ten. Sixteen. Seventeen! Here we are!"

Minnie pulled a gray archival box off the shelf and shooed Alex out of her way. The lid was dusty, but not as dusty as it should have been. She carried the box to a sturdy wooden table near Wadsworth Fairfleet's portrait.

Hands trembling, Minnie removed the lid of the box and began to thumb through the files. Alex knew archival documents had to be handled with care, but it seemed to him that Minnie was being much too slow. "There—it's that one right there!" His fingers itched to grab the file himself, but the glimmer of warning in Asha's eyes checked him.

Finally, Minnie took file number 5 from the box. The first item the archivist drew out of the file was a yellowing piece of paper with a single line of typed text:

May the figs and oranges from our groves—humble though they may be—serve as a symbol of the greater fruits of our collaboration.

Omar Haddad

Director General

His brow scrunched with skepticism, Alex read through the note twice. "I don't get it," he said. "Figs and oranges? Is it a riddle or something?"

Asha shrugged. "It would help if we knew who Omar Haddad was."

"And what he generally directed," Alex added. He set the piece of paper back on the table as Minnie laid out the rest of the items in the file one by one.

There were several old documents that Alex and Asha couldn't interpret—maps with squiggly lines and labels, lists written in old-fashioned cursive handwriting. Alex turned his attention to something he *could* understand: a black-and-white photograph of a desert excavation site.

The photograph was strikingly similar to the picture they had of Dr. Fairfleet at Eremos. It featured the same desert landscape, dramatic cliffs, and toppled columns.

The archaeologist in the black-and-white photograph, however, was a very different sort of scholar. He was rakishly handsome, dressed in khakis and boots, his shirtsleeves rolled up—a regular Indiana Jones. The man's smug smile reminded Alex of Quentin Carlisle's. And this archaeologist was standing in front of a familiar artifact . . .

"The Nabataean Zodiac!" Alex exclaimed.

The Zodiac was propped up against a rock. The animal sculptures were sandy and indistinct against the stone wheel, but Asha didn't think that was the reason the Zodiac looked strange to her. There was definitely something not-quite-right about it.

Alex—who had learned his lesson about failing to check the back of things—flipped the photograph over and read the caption:

"*Xavier Fairfleet, Transjordan, 1925.*

Thirty miles from Petra at a bearing of 170 degrees from true north.'"

Alex traced a compass in the air, divided it into 360 degrees in his head, and found roughly where 170 degrees would be with his index finger. "So that's south, right? Or a little bit southeast, I guess."

"Hmm," Minnie hummed, gently puzzled. "I was under the impression that Eremos was north of Petra, though I would have to look it up to be sure."

Asha took the picture of Dr. Fairfleet at Eremos out of her notebook so that she could study the two photographs side by side. "I don't think these were taken at the same site," she told Alex. "Look at the cliffs in the background. At Eremos, you can see the temple edifice carved into the rock. There's nothing like that in the photo of Xavier Fairfleet."

"Maybe it's a different angle?"

"Maybe . . ." But that was when Asha realized what was bothering her about the Zodiac in the photograph from 1925.

"It's not cracked," she said softly.

"What?"

"The Nabataean Zodiac in the Museum of Natural History has all of these cracks running through it because it was supposedly discovered in pieces in the camel chest. But here it looks fine. It's all in one piece."

The pieces were coming together for Alex too. Under different circumstances, he would have been thrilled to see a real-life conspiracy unfold before his eyes, but with everything else that he knew about the case, he felt only a grim sense of disappointment. "Xavier Fairfleet didn't find the Nabataean Zodiac in the camel chest."

"He didn't find it at Eremos at all," Asha said. "He found it at a different excavation site, thirty miles south of Petra."

"Oh dear," Minnie concluded.

The archivist and the detectives felt the full weight of their discovery settle on their shoulders.

"How did the Zodiac end up broken in the camel chest?" Asha asked.

"Perhaps it was an accident, and Xavier Fairfleet needed to hide his mistake," Minnie proposed.

Alex snorted, which was his way of showing just how likely he found this "accident" hypothesis.

"We have to tell Dr. Wright." Asha's spirits sank. "He's going to be so upset. He loves the story of the Nabataean Zodiac."

"The *lie* of the Nabataean Zodiac, you mean," Alex said with a scowl. "Xavier Fairfleet wasn't collaborating with the Jordanians—he was cheating them! I bet Dr. Wright already knows. I bet he wants to cover it up."

"I'm certain he *doesn't*," Minnie replied with such stern reproach that Alex instantly regretted his words. "Asha's right. We need to tell him." The archivist surveyed the stacks, deep in thought. "Let me find a few more files related to the excavations at Eremos over the years, and then we can go find Dr. Wright together."

○—

Shortly after 2:00 p.m., Alex, Asha, and Minnie walked to the Fairfleet Museum of Natural History. Minnie carried file 1925-17-5 and a collection of other Eremos materials in her arms.

When Dr. Wright saw the subdued trio in the door-way of his office, his face went slack. "What's happened? Is it Alistair?"

"No," Minnie said quickly. "We haven't had any more news about Dr. Fairfleet—good or bad. But . . . oh, perhaps you ought to sit down."

Dr. Wright sat down behind his desk. He did not look at all relieved. Asha supposed that people weren't often told to sit down before receiving good news. Minnie took the photograph of Xavier Fairfleet from the file and passed it to the curator.

Dr. Wright's face was somber as he examined it. "What exactly am I looking at?"

"Xavier Fairfleet posing with the Nabataean Zodiac," Asha said. "Read the caption on the back."

Dr. Wright flipped the photograph over and scanned the caption. "This is a mistake. One hundred and seventy degrees? Eremos is *northeast* of Petra."

"That's what I thought at first too, but the compass directions aren't the problem." Minnie set the stack of files on the desk and opened the one on top. "Xavier Fairfleet didn't discover the Zodiac where he said he did. If you look at this inventory from Eremos . . ." Minnie's finger skimmed the list and stopped halfway down the page. "There, you see."

Dr. Wright read the line that she had indicated. "'Chest with camel relief sculpture, sandstone, $4.3 \times 3.1 \times 3.5$ feet, empty.'" He repeated the last word in a hollow voice. "Empty?"

Dr. Wright looked back and forth between the photograph and the inventory list. His expression was that of a driver caught in dense fog—cautious, confused, and a little bit frightened. "I don't understand how any of this can be true. In this picture, the Zodiac is *intact*. You're suggesting that Xavier Fairfleet found the Zodiac somewhere else, broke a priceless artifact into pieces, and put those pieces in an empty chest from Eremos? Why on earth would he do such a thing?"

"We're not sure," Asha began. "Maybe—"

But Alex had spotted the yellowing piece of paper with the cryptic line about figs and oranges in the file. With a flash of inspiration, he interrupted Asha. "He did it because the camel chest came with a free ticket out of the country!"

Snagging the piece of yellow paper from under Minnie's nose, Alex sprinted toward the Hall of Cultural Artifacts. He skidded to a halt in front of the Nabataean Zodiac display. The others caught up a few seconds later. Alex held up the piece of paper from the file so that it lined up with the bottom of the letter on the wall from the Transjordan Department of Antiquities. The color of the paper and the typeface were a perfect match.

This is what the fully reconstructed letter said:

TRANS-JORDAN GOVERNMENT

DEPARTMENT OF ANTIQUITIES

JERASH

12 November 1925

Dear Dr. Xavier Fairfleet,

On behalf of the government of the Emirate of Transjordan and His Highness the Emir Abdullah, the Department of Antiquities extends its respect and sincere gratitude for your invaluable contributions to the excavation at Eremos. To commemorate this discovery, a triumph for the people of Transjordan and the citizens of all nations, we entrust the Fairfleet Institute with the care and curation of the Nabataean Camel Chest, and we offer, with our thanks, the bounty therein.

May the figs and oranges from our groves—humble though they may be—serve as a symbol of the greater fruits of our collaboration.

Omar Haddad
Director General

Alex realized that his mouth was open, and he closed it. He was equal parts impressed and horrified by the audacity of Xavier Fairfleet's plan. He said, "The Department of Antiquities thought they were sending Xavier Fairfleet home with a fancy fruit basket, and instead he smuggled out the Zodiac."

"'The greater fruits of our collaboration,'" Dr. Wright murmured, more to himself than to anyone else. His gaze hardened and, without warning, he turned and stalked back to his office.

Asha and Alex didn't know if they should follow— Dr. Wright clearly wanted to be alone. However, Asha's backpack was still in his office. After a few indecisive minutes, they decided to retrieve it.

They found the curator seated behind his desk, inspecting the Eremos documents. Asha meant to slip in, grab her backpack, and slip out, but her concern for Dr. Wright hooked her behind the ribs and pulled her into the chair across from him. Alex sat down next to her, while Minnie kept a respectful distance outside the office door.

There was a long pause, and then, still looking at the papers, Dr. Wright said, "There is a plaque commemorating Xavier Fairfleet at the entrance to the museum."

"A plaque?" Alex echoed.

"This is an institution dedicated to preserving and honoring the history of the world and of humanity itself, and we have a plaque at the entrance honoring a man who was little more than a vandal, a thief, a smuggler."

"Okay," Alex began. Although Dr. Wright's tone was controlled, Alex sensed he was treading near landmines. "But you can take down the plaque, right?"

Dr. Wright set down the files he was holding and looked up at Alex and Asha. "Yes, we can take down the plaque. And once we do that, what will have changed? Plaque or no plaque, Xavier Fairfleet stole the Nabataean Zodiac. Nothing anyone does will ever unbreak it." The curator's weary disappointment was quickly giving way to anger. "And this isn't just about Eremos. Do you think the Zodiac is the only piece in our collections with a troubling history? Xavier may have gone further than some in his attempts to conceal his criminal actions, but you can be sure he was not the only director to enrich the Museum of Natural History at the expense of those with less power, wealth, or influence."

Neither Alex nor Asha knew what to say to this. They each felt, in their own way, that the magic of the museum faded a little in that moment. A dim flicker in the lights overhead. A handful of golden dust seeping through the seams in the stone.

"I can accept that Xavier Fairfleet was a liar," Dr. Wright continued bitterly. "It is harder for me to come to terms with the fact that he made every subsequent director of this museum a liar too."

"You didn't know," Asha tried to reassure him— and herself.

"At some point Alistair knew. He knew, and he didn't tell me. And I let myself believe this *fairy tale* about international collaboration. I cared so much about the reputation of the museum and all of the good we strive to do that I failed in my responsibility to redress the harms. My entire career—" Dr. Wright's voice broke, and he fell silent.

Alex had a sudden, horrible premonition of Dr. Wright crying. It had been bad enough seeing Minnie cry, but the stoic curator was a different kind of adult entirely. Alex would sooner expect tears from the stuffed iguana on display in the museum.

To Alex's tremendous relief, Dr. Wright did not cry. He cleared his throat and gathered the frayed shreds of his composure. "May I hold on to these files for a while?" he asked Minnie. "I need some time to think."

They all recognized that they had been dismissed. As Asha picked up her backpack, Minnie replied, "Take as long as you need. If I find anything else in the archives, I'll let you know."

Dr. Wright nodded, but he was looking at the picture of Xavier Fairfleet again; the distance between the detectives and the director behind the desk had increased by thousands of miles and a hundred years.

Alex and Asha declined Minnie's offer to drive them home. They walked down the streets of Northbrook in silence. Sunlight streamed through the trees, and the laughter of other children floated to them on the breeze. Asha didn't understand how anyone could be laughing just now.

"Well, that sucked." Alex kicked a pebble and sent it clattering down the sidewalk. "No. You know what? This whole case sucks. Everything we've figured out is terrible. Dr. Fairfleet might lose his memory, Dr. Ito paints forgeries, and Dr. Wright's professional ideals have been shattered into more pieces than the Zodiac."

"And we're no closer to finding out where Dr. Fairfleet is," Asha added miserably.

"Like I said, it all sucks!" Alex stopped in the middle of the sidewalk, resolved. His face took on a hard angularity in the patterned shadows of the leaves. "Tomorrow I'm going to talk to Dr. Ito, and then I'm going to the police. I think this is a stupid game. I quit."

Alex half expected Asha to contradict him or try to talk him down. She didn't.

"I'll look over all our notes one more time tonight to see if we missed anything," she said. "We can meet up tomorrow at noon and go to the police together."

Asha held out a hand. Alex shook it. The moment seemed to require formal agreement, and detectives didn't pinkie swear.

As they continued their march home, the late afternoon melted into a glorious golden evening. But neither Asha nor Alex—faced as they were with the injustice of the world in general and of detective work in particular—could appreciate the beauty of the mellow twilight.

CHAPTER 11

OF FEATHERS AND FROGS

Friday, July 14th

Alex arrived at the Museum of Art the next morning just as the doors opened to the public. The attendant—a bleary-eyed college student—blinked in surprise when the shorter-than-average twelve-year-old pushed past her and strode into the lobby with all the confidence of a military general.

"I need to speak to Dr. Ito," he said.

"To Dr. Ito?" The attendant blinked again.

"Never mind." Alex pointed himself toward the administrative staircase. "I know where to find her."

"Hey, you're not allowed to go up there," the attendant drawled.

Alex ignored her warning. What did it really mean not to be allowed somewhere when no one was going to stop him?

When he arrived at Dr. Ito's office, he found the director on the phone. She gave him a hassled glance and gestured for him to shut the door—all while carrying on a conversation in flawless French. At least, Alex assumed it was flawless. And he assumed it was French. The languages Alex liked best were for communicating with computers.

Seeing that Alex was still in the hallway, Dr. Ito raised an open-palmed hand—the universal signal for *five more minutes*. Alex could wait five minutes. He parked himself in the doorway.

Evidently, this was not what Dr. Ito had in mind. "Pardon. Un moment, s'il vous plaît," she said to the person on the phone. She walked to the door and gave Alex a steady, steel-edged stare. "When I tell you that I need five minutes, Mr. Foster, I mean five minutes without an eavesdropping amateur detective hovering about."

"It's fine. I don't speak French," Alex said.

Dr. Ito shut the door in his face. It wasn't quite a slam, but it was close.

Rebuffed but not deterred, Alex made his way down the back staircase and wandered through the modern art wing, lost in thoughts as abstract as the colorful paintings on the wall. Eventually he found himself in front of the infamous *Grenouille de l'étang*. Alex glared at the disjointed frog.

"This is all your fault," Alex told the painting.

La Grenouille de l'étang did not reply, but the frog's stuck-out tongue seemed like an insult.

The small informative placard next to the painting caught his attention, and he paused to read it. Reading museum captions was not usually Alex's style. Asha liked to read such things; Alex preferred to *experience* art—or, in a pinch, to have Asha give him a shorthand account of whatever she had read. Today, however, he was angry at Madame Grenouille and determined to know his enemy.

The caption summarized most of what Alex and Asha already knew:

La Grenouille de l'étang, *or* **The Pond Frog,** *is the earliest and most celebrated masterpiece of the elusive artist known as Le Merle. Painted in*

1982, it was initially displayed at the Centre Pompidou in Paris. After an unusual hiatus in private collections, the painting was recovered by the Fairfleet Institute in 2005 and has been a centerpiece of the collection ever since.

As soon as Alex read the paragraph, he knew something was wrong with it. He just didn't know what. It was the worst sort of irritating, like a pine needle stuck in his shoe or an itch between his shoulder blades that he couldn't quite reach. He read the paragraph three more times, hoping the problem would become clear. In the middle of the fourth read-through, he was startled out of his thoughts by Dr. Ito, who had arrived while he was otherwise occupied.

"What can I do for you this morning, Mr. Foster?" the director asked.

Alex straightened up and put on his most professional detective face. "I need to tell you something important, Dr. Ito."

"Well then?"

Alex looked at the impeccably dressed, impossibly poised woman in front of him and tried to imagine her in her art-school days—a rebellious young artist driven to forgery. And then, suddenly, he had it: the solution to the problem with the caption. The scratch to his itch. He stared right past Dr. Ito's head as the answer solidified.

"Are you all right?" Dr. Ito's brow wrinkled with a combination of impatience and concern. "You look like a model for Edvard Munch."

"I don't know what that means—no time to talk now!" Alex's mind was racing at a hundred miles per hour. The soles of his shoes gripped the ground, ready to send him running at a hundred and one. "I'll explain everything later, but you already know . . . you know?"

"Do I?" Dr. Ito asked.

But Alex was already halfway down the hall. He desperately needed to find Asha.

While Alex was sorting things out at the Museum of Art, Asha was sulking. She had been through the entire notebook twice without discovering a single new lead. She agreed with Alex that the time had come to throw in the towel, to pack up the circus, to turn in their guns and badges—in theory anyway. In practice, Asha hated giving up on a good puzzle. To remind herself why they had decided to quit the case in the first place, she went to the Museum of Natural History to check on Dr. Wright.

It was a Friday morning, so the museum was more crowded—or at least less empty—than usual. Asha wished for a moment that everyone would leave her favorite place alone and then felt guilty for making such a selfish wish. What was the museum for if not to be shared with others?

Dr. Wright was in his office; so was Minnie Mayflower. Their hushed discussion ended abruptly when they saw Asha at the door, leading her to suspect that she and Alex may have been the topic of conversation.

"Come in," Dr. Wright said, gesturing for her to enter. He seemed to be in better spirits than he had been the previous afternoon. "Ms. Mayflower is here to collect some of the archival materials she lent me."

"Oh." Asha took a seat next to Minnie, feeling self-conscious. "I wanted to see if you were okay."

Dr. Wright's eyes softened at the corners. "Thank you, Miss Singh. I won't deny that learning the true history of the Zodiac was a disappointment, but I am, as one might say, okay." He straightened the neat piles of paperwork on his desk. "I have contacted the Jordan Museum and the Department of Antiquities. They will be pleased to work with us on repatriating the Nabataean Zodiac—that is, sending it home. I've also decided to begin a review of the origins of all our cultural artifacts, beginning," he emphasized, "with those acquired under the leadership of Xavier Fairfleet."

"That all sounds good." Behind Asha's tentative observation was an unspoken follow-up question: *So then why do you still sound sorry?*

The director let out a subdued sigh. "I'm glad you think so. I doubt the Waverly College board will agree. It's possible that I just signed my own resignation letter. Certainly I will never be a serious contender for the chairmanship of the Institute now."

"You don't know that," Minnie said, but her uncertain tone implied that she didn't know either.

"I must do what I think is right," Dr. Wright replied with more conviction. "And though I can't read all of Alistair's motives, I believe that he will approve. Would approve, if he . . ."

Dr. Wright was spared having to finish this ominous sentence, as a tinny rendition of the Queen of the Night's aria rang out from his breast pocket.

"Excuse me." Dr. Wright took his phone out of his pocket and silenced it. "It's my wife, Martha. I'll call her back."

"*The Magic Flute!*" Asha cried, pointing a dramatic finger at the curator. "It was you!"

Dr. Wright looked nonplussed. "What was I?"

"The intruder at the Fairfleet Mansion!"

"Intruder?" Dr. Wright scoffed. "That's quite rich, considering I have a key to Alistair's home, while you and Mr. Foster were forced to flee out of a back window."

"Asha, you didn't!" The disappointment in Minnie's voice made Asha wince, but she steeled herself against the guilt trip.

"We had to, Minnie! For the sake of the investigation. You both know what Alex and I were looking for." She fixed an inquisitor's glare on Dr. Wright. "What were *you* looking for?"

"If you must know," Dr. Wright said, with just a touch of offended dignity, "I was looking for the Fairfleet Charter."

In fact, Asha hadn't given the charter any real thought in days—it was one more dead end in her notebook—but she couldn't very well admit that to Minnie and Dr. Wright. Recovering her footing, she said, "You think Dr. Fairfleet took the charter?"

"Only he and Ms. Mayflower knew the combination to the safe in the archives, and, as far as I am aware, only Alistair knew what was in the blasted document that made it worth keeping in a safe in the first place."

"Did you find it?"

"I should ask you the same question. By the time I reached Alistair's office, all I found was an empty safe." He reconsidered his statement. "Well, that's not *all* I found." Dr. Wright let out a noise that might have been a puff of amusement or a huff of disapproval. He reached under his desk and withdrew Alex's neon-striped sneaker. "Tell me, did Mr. Foster's carriage turn back into a pumpkin before he got home?"

Asha accepted the sneaker with a sidelong look at Minnie. "Alex will be happy to have this back. They're his favorite pair."

Lost in her own musings, Minnie didn't seem to care about the rogue sneaker at all. "Whoever is behind Dr. Fairfleet's disappearance—that person has the charter. Mark my words."

"Consider them marked." There was a shadow of suspicion behind Dr. Wright's level gaze.

"I do wish I could remember the bit about the succession of the chairmanship in the absence of a Fairfleet heir."

Dr. Wright huffed again, and this time there was no mistaking his derision. "The whole matter of the Fairfleet heir is absurd! If Alistair had been sensible, he would have thrown the charter to the legal wolves years ago."

Now it was Minnie's turn to look suspicious; however, the young archivist did not wear suspicion naturally. She shook it off her shoulders and let it fall to the floor. "So, what was in Dr. Fairfleet's personal safe if not the Fairfleet Charter?" she asked.

Asha reached for her notebook and removed the blue-gray feather from its home between the pages. She placed it on Dr. Wright's desk. "Just this feather. We don't know what it means. We don't even know what kind of bird it's from."

Minnie picked up the feather with childlike delight. "I think I can help! This feather once belonged to a great blue heron!"

Asha and Dr. Wright both stared at her.

"How do you know that?" Asha asked.

"If I knew you were interested in ornithology, I would have invited you to go birding with me!" Dr. Wright exclaimed.

"I'm not much of a birder," Minnie admitted. "When I was a little girl, my mother and I used to vacation on one of the local lakes every summer. There were blue heron nesting grounds near the marshes. I was captivated by them—I could have told you anything you wanted to know about the great blue heron."

Dr. Wright stood up to look at his bookshelves. He took down a large tome titled *Birds of Northbrook*. After consulting the glossary, he turned to the page dedicated to the great blue heron. There was a beautiful full-page illustration of the bird opposite the text.

"It says here that the only blue heron nesting grounds in the general Northbrook area are at Lake Alborg," Dr. Wright said. "I believe that's about twenty minutes outside of town. The Fairfleet family owns all of the land around the lake."

Lake Alborg. Where had Asha heard that name before? She felt as though she were reaching for a light switch in the dark. She knew where it was meant to be on the wall—she just couldn't quite find it.

Minnie, on the other hand, recognized the name at once. "Lake Alborg!" She beamed. "Yes, of course! There was a lovely lake house where we always stayed. A big porch. Wide windows overlooking the water." Her blue eyes grew misty with nostalgia.

"I think you must be mistaken," Dr. Wright said. "Lake Alborg was never developed. Waverly College tried to purchase some of the land from the Fairfleet estate several years back, but Alistair refused. You might find herons, but you won't find any houses."

"I can assure you I am *not* mistaken." Minnie remained polite yet adamant. "I loved that lake house. It was on the far side of the lake, I remember. We had to hike an abandoned trail to get there."

Dr. Wright shrugged—a gesture that paradoxically captured both his unwillingness to fight this battle and his unwillingness to cede any ground—and passed Minnie *Birds of Northbrook* so that she could read the description.

And then Asha found the light switch.

She leapt to her feet. Half of her brain wanted to shout "Eureka!" and the other half wanted to shout "Aha!" What came out was a strangled *"Aheek!"*

"Are you quite all right, Miss Singh? You look like a taxidermy trout."

"I— Stay here!" Asha commanded. She heard how rude she sounded and hastily corrected herself. "I mean, please don't go too far! I'll be right back!"

And with that, she dashed out of Dr. Wright's office and sped through the halls of the Museum of Natural History. She desperately needed to find Alex.

Alex ran out of the Museum of Art and toward the Museum of Natural History just as Asha ran out of the Museum of Natural History and toward the Museum of Art. As luck or fate or maybe coincidence would have it, they met in the middle, right in front of the Fairfleet Center for the Performing Arts.

Alex was red-faced and panting. Asha was still catching her breath as she said, "You'll never believe what I figured out."

"Wait, me first!" Alex cut in. "I've got something *incredible* to tell you."

"I know where Dr. Fairfleet is."

Alex stared at her for a beat. "Fine. You first," he said sourly. He had a full house in hand, but Asha had just played a royal flush. What could he do?

"The feather from the safe came from a blue heron. They have nesting grounds at Lake Alborg, which is on land owned by the Fairfleet family outside of Northbrook."

"That's a new lead!" Alex said.

"I'm not finished." Asha's dark eyes gleamed with triumph. "I thought the name sounded familiar. I had just been through all of our notes, and then I remembered . . ." Asha pulled her notebook out of her backpack and flipped to the original message from Dr. Fairfleet. "Look at the email: sent from a no-reply address at ALB.org."

"Alborg. Son of a biscuit!"

"I'm betting there's a house on that lake," she continued. "Minnie thinks she stayed there as a kid. It must have been built by the Fairfleets."

"Hang on." Alex shook his head, trying to sort through the jumbled bits of information rattling around in his skull. "Why would Minnie have stayed at a house owned by the Fairfleet family?"

"I don't know."

"The fact that Minnie knows about Lake Alborg at all can't be a good thing." Some of the rattling pieces were starting to fall into place, and Alex didn't like the pattern they were forming. "Dr. Ito and Carlisle share a secret that needs to come out. Dr. Wright should be the one to take over as chairman of the Institute. So that leaves Minnie. And if Minnie knows about a secret Fairfleet lake house . . ."

"If Minnie had kidnapped Dr. Fairfleet and was hiding him in a secret lake house, she wouldn't have told me and Dr. Wright about it," Asha said. It felt strange to be defending Minnie from Alex's accusations and not the other way around. "Besides, Minnie isn't the only remaining suspect."

Asha turned the page and showed Alex their original "enclosed clue"—the list of suspects in the investigation. After their very first meeting with Dr. Wright, she had added Dr. Fairfleet's name to the list. "It's the simplest solution. It always has been. It would be *just like* Dr. Fairfleet to sit in his lake house, planning everything from afar."

"But *why*?" Alex demanded. "The message explicitly says that one of the other directors is responsible for his disappearance."

Asha scrunched up her face and let out a frustrated stream of air. "That's fuzzy language," she countered. "You're the one who's always saying we need to trust our instincts. Is your gut telling you that either Minnie or Dr. Wright would want to hurt Dr. Fairfleet?"

"No, it's not. But then what did Dr. Fairfleet mean in his letter?"

Before they could begin to hypothesize, they were interrupted by a rich, clipped, and very unwelcome voice. "Well, if it isn't Sam and Samantha Spade."

"Carlisle," Alex growled. It was not so much a greeting as a mild profanity.

"Making good progress on the case, are we?" the artistic director of the FCPA asked, making it perfectly clear that he didn't care whether they had made any progress at all.

"As a matter of fact, we *have* made progress. We've got a pretty good idea where Dr. Fairfleet is." Asha took a bold step forward to block Carlisle's way. "*And* Alex just came from talking to Dr. Ito. Soon her secret will be out, and then you'll be on the hook for your little blackmail scheme."

"I'd say twenty thousand dollars constitutes more than a 'little' blackmail scheme. Anyway, we'll see about all that. I wouldn't bet against Prudence Ito's instinct for self-preservation." Carlisle glanced at his watch. "Much as I'd love to stay and chat, I have an appointment at the archives. Let's hope that dearest Minerva finds these old programs more interesting than I do."

It took Alex a moment to process what the artistic director had said. "Who's Minerva?"

"Ms. Mayflower, of course. Disney's most boring princess."

"Minnie's full name is Minerva?" The gears were turning in Alex's brain now, and he could tell that the machinery had switched on for Asha too.

"Minerva is the Roman name for Athena," she whispered to Alex.

"I know that!"

Asha chanted the last clue of the treasure hunt like a magic spell: *"Goddess of wisdom and strategy too, my greatest regret is giving up you."*

The detectives fell silent as they searched each other's eyes for the truth they had stumbled upon. Carlisle, for once, did not break their focus with a snide remark.

"The photo of Minnie and the directors in Dr. Fairfleet's bedroom," Asha said.

"Minnie's scholarship at Waverly College. Her job at the Institute when her mom got sick," Alex added.

"King Lear."

"The lake house."

"The Fairfleet Charter."

Silence again. Carlisle looked from one young detective to the other. "I was doing a spectacular job of ignoring Alistair's game of *Clue*, but it would take a lot more self-control than I possess to turn a blind eye to *that* little performance." The director straightened his linen vest. "Out with it. What dramatic conclusion have you reached?"

"All in good time, my dear Watson," Alex said, pleased to see Carlisle scowl in annoyance.

"Would you care to join us and the other directors for a little hike around Lake Alborg tomorrow morning?" Asha asked.

"I think it should be obvious that I would *not*," Carlisle replied.

"Well, too bad!" A smile, something between a smirk and a grin, was spreading across Alex's face. "If you want to know what we know, you'll meet us at the Museum of Natural History at eight a.m. sharp tomorrow morning."

The detectives were so preoccupied by the ramifications of their discovery, so caught up in preparations for the next morning, that Alex completely forgot to tell Asha about what he had learned at the art museum. When he remembered halfway through brushing his teeth for bed, he nearly swallowed a mouthful of toothpaste. He stared at himself in the mirror, a trail of minty foam dribbling down his chin, as he thought about what to do next.

He couldn't text Asha; this was the sort of news that needed to be shared in person. He considered holding on to the big reveal and saving a moment of glory for himself . . . but only briefly. Alex had learned a lot over the course of the case. For instance, he'd learned to tie double knots in his laces before breaking into mansions and to beware of smug archaeologists bearing gifts. Finally and foremost, he had learned that true partnership was all about communication.

Alex spat out his toothpaste, splashed water on his face, and made up his mind. As he padded back to his bedroom, he listened to make sure the house was silent and sleepy. The window near his bed opened over the garage. He climbed out onto the shingled roof. From there, he just had to shimmy down the gutter to the ground below.

With the grass dewy beneath his bare feet and the moon lighting his way, Alex set off down the street to talk with Asha.

Asha lay in bed as the clock ticked toward midnight. The fifteenth of July. She was wide awake with the sort of excitement usually reserved for important holidays. Just as she was contemplating turning on her lamp and reading for a while, Asha was startled by the tap of a small stone against her bedroom window. She raised the sash to see Alex standing in her backyard in his pajamas.

"Psst, Asha!" Alex hissed in the loudest whisper imaginable. "Come down. I have to tell you what I learned about the case!"

"Now?" Asha asked. "It's so late!"

"Justice doesn't sleep!" Alex replied.

Asha hesitated . . . but only briefly. She had learned a few lessons of her own over the past two weeks. For instance, she'd learned never to leave a jigsaw puzzle unfinished and not to confuse her Greek and Roman goddesses. Above all, she had learned that there was a time to hold true to her ideals and a time to bend the rules a bit.

Asha snuck out of her house and into the warm night to meet with Alex.

CHAPTER 12

THE LAKE HOUSE

Saturday, July 15th, 8:00 a.m.

On the morning of July 15th, the weather decided to cooperate fully with the investigation. The sky was a stunning blue, dotted here and there with lamb's-wool clouds. A sweet breeze from the west kept the day from becoming too hot.

Alex, Asha, and all four directors of the Fairfleet Institute were taking in the fine weather by hiking around Lake Alborg in search of a secret lake house. Dr. Wright had driven, as his SUV was the only vehicle large enough for all six of them. They parked in a small lot overlooking a nature preserve—heron nesting grounds, in fact—and began their trek. There was, as Minnie had mentioned, an abandoned

Forest Service trail around the perimeter of the lake, though it was so muddy and overgrown that calling it a trail at all seemed generous.

None of the directors were prepared for a morning outdoors. Minnie managed well enough in a light, floral sundress. Dr. Wright, at least, had worn sensible shoes. Dr. Ito might have dressed down for the occasion, but Asha wasn't sure how to tell a fancy silk scarf from an everyday one. It was Carlisle who fared the worst in the lakeside woods. The little holes in his leather shoes filled up with mud, he was sweating through his vest, and he kept swatting at the gnats that were attracted to his cologne. He looked miserable, to Alex's undisguised delight.

On and on they marched as the morning grew late and the sunlight warmed the shining surface of the lake. Asha was starting to wonder if she might have been wrong about Lake Alborg—perhaps they were about to stumble upon an entire school of red herring—when the dense undergrowth thinned, and the trees gave way to a wide clearing. In the clearing was a beautiful A-frame house with a wraparound porch and floor-to-ceiling windows facing the water.

"I told you there was a house!" Minnie exclaimed. "It's just as I—" But she didn't finish her sentence. Everyone was staring at the house.

On the wide porch was a table laid out for seven. Next to the table was an oversized Adirondack chair. And in this Adirondack chair sat none other than Dr. Alistair Fairfleet.

Asha's shoulders slumped with relief as Alex began to laugh like an unhinged parrot. Dr. Fairfleet looked plump and healthy. His shirtsleeves were rolled up, his white beard was neatly trimmed, and his glasses gleamed in the sunlight.

"Hullo!" he said cheerfully, raising a glass of iced tea and beckoning them all onto the porch. He checked his pocket watch. "My, you are punctual, aren't you!"

Dr. Ito was the first of the directors to respond. She strode across the clearing in her perfect shoes, snatched the glass of iced tea from Dr. Fairfleet's hands, and threw its contents right in his face.

"Alistair Montgomery Fairfleet!" Dr. Ito brandished the now empty glass. "Of all the half-witted, idiotic— Do you have any idea how much trouble you've caused? How *worried* we've been?"

Dr. Fairfleet removed his glasses so that he could mop his tea-splattered face with a handkerchief. "I'm happy to see you, too, Prudence."

"Don't be glib, Alistair."

"I wouldn't dream of it." Dr. Fairfleet gave Alex and Asha a twinkly-eyed smile before turning his attention to the other directors. "John, I am sorry about my half-witted, idiotic scheme, as Prudence so aptly described it. I hope that everything will be made clear soon. Quentin—I wasn't sure whether to expect you or not, but I set a place for you just in case." The chairman's demeanor changed as his gaze fell on Minnie. "And Minerva, how are you?"

"I'm well enough." Minnie seemed flustered by the seriousness with which he addressed her. "Captain Nemo is well too. He's been staying with me."

"Of course he has." Dr. Fairfleet studied her face and then asked Asha and Alex, "I take it you haven't told them yet?"

"Not yet," Asha said.

Dr. Wright addressed the white-haired Dr. Fairfleet as he might a student at a disciplinary hearing. "I think it's time we heard whatever it is you have to tell us. All of it."

"So you shall, John. But first, I think some lunch is in order." Dr. Fairfleet gestured toward the table. "The sandwiches are from Behrman's Deli. I placed the order anonymously, and Mr. Behrman dropped them off at the scenic overlook, no questions asked. A true Northbrook gem, Behrman's!"

The directors sat down at the table. None of them were inclined to eat. To make up for their meager appetites, Alex polished off one of every kind of sandwich: honey ham and mustard, roast beef and horseradish mayonnaise, and hummus vegetable. It would have been rude not to. Wondering what would happen next, Asha sipped her iced tea. Her throat was dry.

When Alex had finished eating and the others had stopped picking at their sandwiches, Dr. Fairfleet turned to the young detectives. "Now then, perhaps the A&A Detective Agency would be so good as to shed some light on this case."

"What?" Asha asked, rattled. "But we didn't prepare anything. We thought that you . . ."

Dr. Fairfleet's blue eyes danced. "And deprive my favorite sleuths of their moment in the spotlight? I wouldn't dream of it!"

Asha's face froze over like a pond in February. Alex recognized that look; he had seen it plenty of times when Asha was called on at school. She always knew the answer, but she resented feeling like it was her responsibility to rescue the class.

"Well," Alex said, sifting through the threads of the mystery, wondering where to begin. "In the end, Dr. Fairfleet told us most of what we needed to know in his very first letter."

Asha decided she couldn't let Alex shoulder the burden alone, though Alex wouldn't have minded. "*Two of you share a secret that has been kept in the shadows for too long,*" she quoted. "First, we discovered that Carlisle was blackmailing Dr. Ito."

Minnie let out a little sigh, which communicated that she was disappointed in Carlisle but not entirely surprised. Carlisle wore an expression of perfect indifference.

"We didn't know what Carlisle could possibly have on Dr. Ito that would force her to pay him twenty thousand dollars," Asha continued, "until we discovered her old sketchbook. When we saw her sketches of *La Grenouille de l'étang,* we concluded that the prized modern masterpiece of the Fairfleet collection was a forgery."

"Preposterous!" Dr. Wright cut in. "I've never heard such a ridiculous accusation in my life. Surely there's been some mistake, Prudence."

The director of the art museum maintained a stubborn silence.

"We'll come back to that soon," Alex said, poker-faced. "Dr. Fairfleet also said that one of you would replace him as chair of the Institute. The obvious successor should have been Dr. Wright. Minnie isn't qualified for the position, and she never wanted it in the first place. And Dr. Wright is the only person in the world who loves the Museum of Natural History and the Institute as much as Dr. Fairfleet. But there was also the inconvenient problem of the missing Fairfleet Charter."

"And then we finally figured out the last clue in the museum treasure hunt. Dr. Fairfleet wasn't talking about the bust of Athena; he was trying to tell us that the thing he most regretted giving up was *Minerva*," explained Asha.

Alex spoke directly to Minnie. "You told us that Dr. Fairfleet's retirement would be thorny. What if it's going to be even thornier because of something—or someone—that he had to give up thirty years ago when he went to Eremos?"

"It would explain a lot," Asha noted. "Like why Dr. Fairfleet chose *King Lear* for the archival puzzle."

"Or why he keeps a picture of you and the directors with the other family photographs in his lonely mansion," added Alex.

Utterly bewildered, Minnie glanced from Alex to Asha to Dr. Fairfleet.

"Don't you get it, Minnie? You're—"

Asha silenced Alex by jabbing her elbow into his ribs and shaking her head. This was not their secret to reveal. They all turned to Dr. Fairfleet.

"You're my daughter, Minerva."

Minnie swayed a little in her seat. "I'm sorry," she said faintly. "I think I must have misheard you."

Dr. Ito put a kind, steadying hand on Minnie's back. "You heard him just fine."

"I don't understand. My mother told me that my father was dead."

"And I don't blame her for that. Not anymore. Please allow me to explain."

Asha, who was seated next to Dr. Fairfleet, noticed that his hands were shaking, though he kept them hidden under the table.

Dr. Fairfleet waited until Minnie gave a feeble nod to continue. "I met your mother one summer when she was working at Waverly College. Neither of us saw our relationship as anything serious. We found out Ella was pregnant with you the same week that I received my research grant to go to Jordan for two years. I had been planning this sabbatical for months, and my work meant so much to me. I . . . Well, I chose Eremos." Dr. Fairfleet watched Minnie closely to see how she would respond, but the archivist's face was as white as a blank piece of paper.

"I knew I had made the wrong choice as soon as I arrived overseas. I regretted missing your birth, your first steps, your first words. When I returned to Northbrook, you were a toddler, and your mother wanted nothing at all to do with me. I had already given up my chance to be your father in her eyes."

Dr. Ito gave a little sniff that seemed to suggest she was not entirely unsympathetic to Ella Mayflower's point of view.

"I watched you grow up from afar. Supported you financially as Ella would let me, though she was a proud, stubborn woman. The only real gift she ever accepted from me was the use of this lake house for your summer vacations. I wanted to tell you so many times." Dr. Fairfleet raised his hands—trembling, empty hands.

No one at the table dared so much as blink until Minnie, whose cheeks were now damp with tears, spoke. "I thought that my mother was the only family I had, and when she died, I thought that I had no one at all." There was a stinging barb of accusation in her voice.

"I told myself that I was doing the right thing when I chose to abide by the wishes of the woman I had wronged, but I . . ." The end of Dr. Fairfleet's explanation faded into silence.

"That's—nonsense," Minnie said, the sting in her voice now a full-fledged bite. Asha had the distinct impression that Minnie had stopped herself from uttering a much harsher expletive in front of her and Alex. "I'm sorry, but that's just nonsense!"

Minnie looked older than she had a moment ago—older, and much harder. It took Alex a second to realize she was *angry*. He had never seen Minnie angry before. Not when he buried her class notes in the backyard. Not when he took baby Ollie to the grocery store and left him in the produce aisle hoping that someone would purchase him for $2.99 a pound. But there was no mistaking the anger that blanched the young archivist's cheeks, thinned her lips, and darkened her eyes.

"You can lie to yourself all you want," Minnie continued, "but the truth is you're a coward. You didn't want to face my mother, or you weren't ready for the responsibility of fatherhood, or both. And now that my mother is dead, instead of coming to talk to me, you staged this ridiculous mystery to avoid the conversation and soften the blow!" Minnie's verbal attack grew steadily louder as she hit her stride. Dr. Fairfleet shrank from the onslaught. "How could you possibly delude yourself into thinking that any of this was fair? To tell me in front of everyone? To let Dr. Wright discover the truth about the Nabataean Zodiac in an archival box? You—you!" Minnie was grasping at straws now but not quite ready to quit. "You didn't even arrange proper care for Captain Nemo!" She drew a shuddering breath. "I'm sick to death of this job and the Institute and this town and all of the *nonsense*"—again, Asha substituted a stronger word in her mind—"that goes along with them!"

Her tirade complete, Minnie stood breathing heavily while she awaited Dr. Fairfleet's response. But Dr. Fairfleet had no response. With a huff, Minnie picked up her cardigan and stalked off the porch toward the woods. Alex and Asha exchanged alarmed glances and hopped up to go after her. So, to their surprise, did Dr. Wright.

They followed Minnie to a clearing in a circle of pine trees. The ground was covered in a soft layer of pine needles and periwinkle flowers, and the blue of the lake was just visible through the sweeping boughs. Minnie sat down on a tree stump. Her posture drooped. The anger had faded from her face, but she still seemed older, somehow.

She looked up as Alex, Asha, and Dr. Wright padded over the bed of needles and flowers to join her. "I suppose I made a fool of myself back there," she said with a wan smile.

"Trust me, Ms. Mayflower, you are not the one who looks foolish in all of this," Dr. Wright replied.

"I never would have imagined that someone could yell at Dr. Fairfleet," Asha said. "I think he deserved it, though."

"He certainly did." Dr. Wright cleared a patch of brown earth and sat down on the ground next to Alex. It was not a natural position for the dignified director. "I rather envy you, letting him have it like that."

"Are you going to yell at Dr. Fairfleet too?" Alex asked. "About the Zodiac?"

"Oh, I don't know." Dr. Wright took a few pine needles and rolled them between his fingers. "I thought I might, when I first saw him sitting on that porch, but since Ms. Mayflower has effectively called him to task for being a coward, I see no reason to belabor the point. My battle now is with the Fairfleet Institute itself. How do I reconcile my love for this work with the Institute's history and its flaws? Where do we go from here?" Dr. Wright trained his focus back on Minnie and watched her with interest. "And what about you? Where will you go from here?"

"I'm not sure." Minnie sounded weary. "Part of me wants to march back to that house and tell him I don't need or want him in my life. That's what my mother would have done. But if I'm being honest, I think I *do* want him in my life. I'm not prepared to sever the only family connection I have left."

Asha tried to put herself in Minnie's shoes but found that they were not very comfortable; sensing Minnie's loneliness and confusion, she said nothing. Alex, however, put on his most serious adult face to offer his two cents. "If Dr. Fairfleet wants to be a better dad, and if you want him to be a better dad, then I don't think it makes sense to punish him for being a bad dad in the past by pushing him away now. He deserves a chance to try."

Dr. Wright looked both impressed and surprised, which Alex found gratifying and annoying, respectively. "That's quite astute, Mr. Foster. Even, I daresay, wise." Dr. Wright then told Minnie, "The relationship can proceed on your own terms and at your own pace. Alistair knows he owes you that much."

Minnie looked through the trees at the sun glinting off the lake. "We should head back."

"At your own pace," Dr. Wright repeated.

Minnie closed her eyes. "Five more minutes, then."

They waited out the five minutes in perfect silence. A breeze swept through the pine branches while lake water lapped lightly at the shore several meters off. It was very peaceful; even Alex wasn't bored. At the end of the five minutes, Minnie stood up straight and tall. She offered one hand to Alex and the other to Asha to help them to their feet.

Dr. Wright heaved himself up with a grunt. "Is it time?" he asked.

Minnie replied with a calm certainty that seemed to capture the present moment, and the whole mystery leading up to it, and thirty odd years without a father: "It's time."

CHAPTER 13

THE TRUTH, AS THEY SAY, WILL OUT

Saturday, July 15th, 2:00 p.m.

Back at the lake house, the atmosphere that greeted the quartet as they emerged from the woods was tense, to say the least. Asha supposed that Dr. Fairfleet, Dr. Ito, and Quentin Carlisle could hardly be expected to enjoy small talk or lawn games at a time like this. Everyone waited to see what Minnie would do or say next.

Minnie sat down at the table, head up and shoulders back. "Would someone please pass the sandwiches? I think I've found my appetite."

"Minerva—" Dr. Fairfleet began.

"Minnie," the archivist said, meeting his gaze at last. "You can call me Minnie."

It didn't seem like much of a response to Alex, but it clearly meant a great deal to Dr. Fairfleet. His face melted into a puddle of guilt and grief, and his eyes filled with tears. "'When thou dost ask me blessing, I'll kneel down and ask of thee forgiveness. So we'll live, and pray, and sing, and tell old tales, and laugh at gilded butterflies.'"

Carlisle leaned over and said as an aside to Alex, "That's *Lear*. Act five, scene three."

"*Shut. Up*," Alex hissed back.

"Let's not get ahead of ourselves," Minnie said, taking a roast beef sandwich from the platter and daintily wiping horseradish mayonnaise from her fingertips with a napkin. "If this relationship is going to work, it will proceed at *my* pace." She inclined her head toward Dr. Wright. "I think we're a ways from gilded butterflies yet."

"You're absolutely right," Dr. Fairfleet assured her, bowing his white head. "You don't need to decide anything, to *do* anything right now. I know this is a lot to take in. But maybe once you've had some time . . ." The chairman looked past Minnie out at Lake Alborg. The water reflected the sky, which was as brilliantly blue as Dr. Fairfleet's—and Minnie's—eyes.

Dr. Ito picked a splinter off of the table with her elegant fingernails. "You'll forgive me for ruining such a tender family moment, Alistair, but this all seems like a very complicated way of announcing your paternity."

"Ah." Dr. Fairfleet took a cloth from his pocket and wiped clean his glasses, which had gotten a bit foggy with emotion. "Yes, it's time we dealt with that whole business. As you will have gathered from my letter, I have decided to retire."

"The chairman of the Fairfleet Institute cannot simply retire," observed Dr. Wright. "It's a lifetime appointment."

"Nevertheless, retire I shall. Six months ago, I found out that I am in the early stages of cognitive decline," Dr. Fairfleet told them with no trace of self-pity. "My doctor thinks I may have as many as ten good years left. That's a funny number, ten years. A decade seems like a long time until you know it's all you have left." He paused as a fresh breeze ruffled the water and made their napkins flutter across the table. "I've spent my whole life thinking about legacy—about the things we leave behind. I dedicated my career to preserving my family's legacy. The very purpose of the Institute is to curate the cultural inheritance of humanity. But now I look back at my time on this earth, and all I see are other people's stories and histories. The last decade of my life will be my own."

"But what will you do if you're not working?" Asha asked. She couldn't picture Dr. Fairfleet without his books and papers.

"I'd like to travel," Dr. Fairfleet replied. "And I'd like to get to know my daughter. The one goal might serve the other. Although most of my family wealth is tied up in the Institute, I have a sizable personal fortune that ought to be spent. Northbrook will always be home, but it is a complicated place to be a Fairfleet. Easier, perhaps, to discover one's roots at a café in Paris."

"Or a museum in Edinburgh," Minnie said, careful to sound casual, to avoid making promises.

"A true Fairfleet can never resist a good museum," Dr. Fairfleet agreed. He was rewarded with a small smile from Minnie. He returned the smile magnified tenfold and drew in a deep breath of summer air. "Asha, would you mind popping into the kitchen and bringing out the box on the counter?"

Asha did as she was told and returned a moment later with the box in question. It was about the size of a hefty dictionary and made of ivory-colored wood—not painted, but sun-bleached. The lid was inlaid with onyx squares. The box had an unmistakable Fairfleetness about it, a riddle-whispering quality.

She could feel her pulse beating in her palms as she gave the box to Dr. Fairfleet. The chairman began to play with the black squares, which shifted and slid around each other. The box was similar to the sliding tile puzzles that Asha had loved when she was little, but there was no picture to create, no clear frame of reference. She had trouble following the complex pattern of Dr. Fairfleet's movements. He clearly knew what he was doing, however, for at the end of the pattern, there was a crisp click, and the box lid sprang open.

Inside the box was a very old document stamped with the Fairfleet family crest.

"The charter!" Minnie exclaimed. She spun around to face Dr. Wright. "You were right! Dr. Fairfleet had it all along."

"I believe you were the one who said that whoever was behind Alistair's disappearance would have the charter. Since Alistair was behind his own disappearance, it would seem we were both right."

"Well, good. Now we can finally sort out all of this confusion about the Fairfleet heir," Minnie said with brisk optimism.

Asha and Alex waited nervously for the archivist to reach the inevitable destination of her train of thought. When Minnie realized the truth, she recoiled in horror. "Oh . . . no. *I'm* the Fairfleet heir!"

"Congratulations?" Alex offered.

Minnie turned to lash out at Dr. Fairfleet with the panicked desperation of a bird caught in a trap. "But I can't! That is, I won't—you can't make me!"

"No one is going to make you do anything." Dr. Fairfleet started to reach for Minnie's hand but, seeing his daughter's fierce frown, thought better of it. He picked up the charter instead. "I devised this puzzle to reconnect with my daughter. Minnie, you are the *reason* for all of this. *One of you, alas, is responsible for my sudden disappearance.* You are not, therefore, the person I had in mind to succeed me as chair of the Institute."

"Everyone, listen." Dr. Fairfleet swapped out his regular glasses for a pair of reading spectacles. He began scanning the cursive lines of the charter, mumbling as he read: "'The chairmanship is a lifetime appointment. The current head of the Fairfleet family will hold the position until his death, at which point the chairmanship will pass to the oldest eligible Fairfleet heir.'"

"We already knew all that," Alex said, hovering over Dr. Fairfleet's shoulder.

"Yes, yes." The chairman shooed him away. "That's not what I wanted to read to you. Now, where was I . . . 'In the event that the heir is a minor'—no, that's not the one. 'In the event that a younger Fairfleet sibling'—no . . . Aha! Here!" Dr. Fairfleet shook the charter, jabbing his finger at a clause in the middle of the page. Minnie cringed to see the founding document so abused.

Dr. Fairfleet cleared his throat and read without mumbling now. "'In the event that the chairman dies without an acknowledged heir, the remaining directors of the Institute shall select the next chair by nomination, seconding, and unanimous approval.'"

"That would be quite helpful if you were dead," Carlisle noted. "But unfortunately for all of us, you are very much alive, and your heir is sitting right here."

Dr. Fairfleet gave Carlisle a withering stare over the top of his glasses. "Quentin, for once in your life, please be quiet and let me finish." He continued reading: "'In the event that the director is insensible, missing, or otherwise incapacitated for more than five weeks without an acknowledged heir, the remaining directors will select the next chair according to the procedure outlined above.'"

Dr. Fairfleet lowered the charter to address his audience. "Alex," he said. "You seem like the sort of young man who enjoys a good technicality."

"Sure, who doesn't?" Alex shrugged.

"When would you say that Minnie was 'acknowledged' as my daughter?"

"This afternoon, I guess. Right after lunch."

"Very good. And how long was I missing?"

Alex had to think about that one. "Well, you went missing the morning of June tenth, so it's been exactly five weeks." He paused and cracked a smile. "Plus a couple of hours."

"Then it would be fair to say that I was missing without an acknowledged heir for more than five weeks?"

Alex was about to respond, but Dr. Ito preempted him. "We get the point, Alistair. We're not children."

Of course, some of them *were* children, but Alex didn't think it was worth correcting her.

Dr. Ito raised her right hand. "As a director of the Fairfleet Institute, I nominate John Wright as our next chairman."

Minnie let out an excited squeak and raised her hand as well. "I second the nomination."

Dr. Ito glared at the artistic director of the Fairfleet Center for the Performing Arts. "So help me, Carlisle—if you don't cast your vote, I'll see to it that you end up directing youth productions of *The Wizard of Oz* for the rest of your life."

"I am immune to your petty threats, Prudence," Carlisle said, but he raised his hand anyway.

"There you have it, John." Dr. Fairfleet swapped back his regular glasses, clearly pleased with the proceedings. "For a unanimous vote of the directors, you need only to accept the nomination."

But Dr. Wright did not immediately accept. He looked up at the high, sloped roof of the Fairfleet lake house, at the wide windows overlooking the shining water.

"Alistair, you should have told me about Xavier Fairfleet," he said after a span of silence.

"I know I should have. I told myself that I was doing you a favor. I didn't want to drag you into the muck, and I didn't want to jeopardize the reputation of the Institute until I had all of the evidence in hand—but I see now that I was wrong to keep you in the dark for so long." Dr. Fairfleet's tone was matter-of-fact. Asha knew Dr. Wright well enough to understand that he would prefer this sort of candor to a more sentimental apology.

"I'm sending the Nabataean Zodiac back to Jordan," Dr. Wright said. "I've already started the arrangements. There's no point arguing about it now."

"I know that too."

"And I'm beginning a review of our collections. The Zodiac won't be the only piece we lose."

"*I know*, John." Dr. Fairfleet's voice was still measured, but now it carried the faintest trace of desperation. "Do you think you're raising valid objections to your promotion? It is *because of*—not *in spite of*—your ethical instincts that you must be the one to succeed me at the Institute. You've never been given to false modesty. Surely you know you're the best—the only—man for the job."

Dr. Wright was not, in fact, given to false modesty, and his chest swelled a little at the compliment. "But the board," he began.

"Stuff the board!" Dr. Fairfleet proclaimed. "The legacy of the Institute has never belonged to the board! Look here—I can't pretend that this will be an easy transition. Being the chairman of the Fairfleet Institute is a tremendous honor, but it can also be a great burden. The history of the Institute is complex and, as you well know, not always pleasant." Dr. Fairfleet looked down at the charter. "You have earned this position, but unlike me, or even Minnie, you are not obligated to accept the role unless you choose it, burdens and all."

Dr. Wright laid his hands flat on the wood of the table as though seeking to absorb its sun-soaked solidity while he contemplated the choice before him. At last he said, "I've been weighing some words of wisdom I heard earlier this afternoon. I think perhaps that if the Institute can change for the better, and if I want it to be better, it doesn't make sense to turn down this opportunity to make it so."

Alex grinned and poked Asha in the side to remind her whose words of wisdom Dr. Wright had been weighing.

If Dr. Wright saw Alex's reaction, he pretended not to. Instead he continued, "But I have conditions."

"Name them," said. Dr. Fairfleet.

"For the sort of changes I have in mind, I'll need your connections and your support. We've always been partners; I won't be left to clean up this mess alone while you wash your hands of it. You intend to travel through Europe? Good. You can meet with our colleagues at the major European museums to discuss our plan to review our collections and repatriate contested pieces." Dr. Wright waited to make sure that his next words were marked. "And you'll start by talking to the National Archaeological Museum in Greece about the bust of Pallas Athena. *If* she stays in our collection, it won't be because we dodged hard questions."

Dr. Fairfleet seemed surprised and perhaps even unsettled by this speech. It was not, the detectives suspected, what he had in mind for the first year of his retirement. He did not delay for long, however. "You're right, John. Of course you're right. Your conditions are only fair. I'll call Athens first thing Monday morning and start planning the itinerary."

"In that case," Dr. Wright said after another deliberate pause, "I accept the chairmanship. Burdens and all."

"Thank you," Dr. Fairfleet replied—a solemn, earnest admission of gratitude. And the two men shook hands.

Quentin Carlisle had been following this whole exchange with a muted grimace, as though he were watching a bad movie and trying not to offend the friend who had dragged him to it.

"Let me get this straight," he said. "We've all been your pathetic pawns these past few weeks—solving your little puzzles, enduring your insults—all so you could invoke a loophole in your family's charter? Surely you could have just hired a lawyer, or a whole team of lawyers, for that matter!"

"The charter is legally sound. There's nothing my lawyers could have done. Besides, you're the only one I bothered to insult, Quentin."

"What about the solar eclipse?" Asha asked, trying to work out how the timing of an astronomical event could coincide so neatly with the five-week waiting period stipulated in the charter. "Was that just a coincidence?"

Dr. Fairfleet looked a little sheepish. "Not exactly, no. I had the whole plan worked out months ago, but I couldn't quite bring myself to set it all in motion. I was stalling . . . I suppose I have been a coward. The eclipse felt like a signal from the universe, the shot from a cosmic starting pistol. I left that very morning, and I set the rest of the dates accordingly."

"In other words, your timing was as arbitrary as the rest of your insane plotting!" Carlisle was turning red from anger and the heat of the day. "There's no logical reason why everything had to be so cryptic. Not everything is a damn *game!*" He spat out this last word like a chunk of rotten hard-boiled egg.

Dr. Fairfleet sat up straighter in his chair, affronted. "Quentin, I'm afraid there are some things that you and I will never see eye to eye on."

"But did you have to involve the children?" Minnie asked. "They've been so worried."

"Of course, I had to involve them," Dr. Fairfleet said, less affronted but still defensive. "They're the best problem-solvers in Northbrook. How else was I to make sure that you all followed your clues and got here on time?" He cast a guilty glance toward Asha and Alex. "You weren't terribly worried, were you? We read *The Westing Game* together last summer. I thought you'd understand."

"We weren't worried," Alex lied. He reflected and amended his claim. "Well, we were a *little* worried."

"We're still a little worried," Asha said, thinking of Dr. Ellen Price and Dr. Fairfleet's diagnosis.

"I am sorry, then," Dr. Fairfleet conceded. "I can't say that I regret the game itself, but I regret causing you all such alarm. And I regret, John, that I'm leaving you to hire four new directors as your first act as chairman."

"Four?" Carlisle looked as though he'd been bitten by a horsefly.

"Yes, four. He'll have to find his own replacement for the Museum of Natural History. Minnie won't be able to keep up with her responsibilities if she chooses to travel. And as for you and Prudence . . . Really now, Quentin. Forgery and blackmail are both felonies. Surely you didn't think you'd be allowed to keep your positions at the Institute?"

"But Dr. Ito—" Alex began.

The director of the Museum of Art cut him off with a sharp glare and a stern rebuke. "That's enough, Mr. Foster."

Dr. Fairfleet considered this exchange with clear curiosity. "I would like to hear what Alex has to say. Many a mistake might have been avoided by listening to a simple 'but.'"

Alex stared down Dr. Ito with exasperated courage. "You say that *I'm* stubborn, but you're the one who's about to lose the job you love for no reason!"

"Oh, very well," Dr. Ito relented, wrapping herself in her silk shawl, closing herself off like an insect inside a cocoon.

Alex's face lit up. He'd been waiting all day to reveal this part of the mystery that even Dr. Fairfleet didn't seem to know. He really wished he had a prop—a hat or a pipe or something like that. He settled for a stick that he found lying on the porch near the table, a stick that he now pointed at Asha.

"Asha Singh," he said. "Can you tell me the year in which *La Grenouille de l'étang* was painted?"

"1982," Asha said, trying not to laugh at Alex's antics. They had rehearsed their scene the night before, but she was still impressed that he had finally learned how to pronounce the name of the painting.

"Correct!" Alex declared. "And what was the date that was written on Dr. Ito's sketchbook?"

"1980."

"Correct again!"

Asha opened her eyes wide and lifted her hands in mock confusion. "But then how did she . . ."

"How indeed!" Alex's timing wasn't quite right, but he made up for it with a dramatic flourish of his stick. "I'll tell you how! Because the drawings in the sketchbook weren't studies *of* the painting; they were studies *for* the painting!" He brought the stick swishing around in a great arc and stopped when the tip was mere inches from Dr. Ito's face. The museum director did not blink.

"Ladies and gentlemen, Dr. Ito could not have forged the work of Le Merle because she *is* Le Merle!"

Alex was expecting a more dramatic reaction than he got. Only Minnie, ever-obliging, gasped. Carlisle almost knocked over his glass of iced tea, but a baffled Dr. Wright caught it. Dr. Fairfleet began to laugh, his mirth both rich and clear. Dr. Ito looked as though she would rather have been anywhere else at that moment than at Lake Alborg on a sunny summer afternoon.

Dr. Fairfleet stopped chortling long enough to address the art director. "Prudence, I can't remember the last time

I was this surprised. It's good for the soul, a bit of shock. I'm sorry that I ever doubted you. I've always admired the work of Le Merle."

"Then you're a fool," Dr. Ito retorted. "No one would have cared a lick about those paintings if it weren't for the anonymous French artist the world invented. I've spent half my life trying to put as much distance between myself and Le Merle as possible."

This last sentence solicited a dry cough from Dr. Wright.

"If you've something to say, John, just say it." Dr. Ito glowered at him.

"I would merely point out that the Museum of Art wouldn't be half so successful if it weren't for that funny frog. And I imagine it is Le Merle who paid for your shoes and your scarves and your fancy car."

"He also paid for a little villa in the south of France, which is where I'll be headed as soon as word gets out."

"Word won't get out," Dr. Wright said with an easy sense of authority befitting the new chairman of the Fairfleet Institute. "I don't know if the Museum of Art can afford to lose the mystery of Le Merle. I am certain, however, that it can't afford to lose Dr. Prudence Ito."

The storm clouding Dr. Ito's expression began to subside. "I would, of course, prefer not to leave the Institute during this period of transition."

"Naturally," said Dr. Wright.

Carlisle seemed perturbed by this recent series of revelations. His face had gone from red to clammy pink. A strand of hair had made a daring escape from its gelled comrades and was dangling sweatily in his eyes.

"You paid me twenty thousand dollars to keep quiet about a crime you didn't commit?"

"No, Carlisle. I paid you twenty thousand dollars to shut up about the painting so that I would never have to face a situation like *this*." Dr. Ito glared at Carlisle and then at everyone else seated around the table, including—perhaps mostly—at Alex.

"However," she continued, "now that the cat's out of the bag, I will be expecting my money back."

Carlisle balked. "But I don't have it anymore."

Dr. Ito turned her head toward the wretched man. "What do you mean, you don't have it anymore? How did you manage to lose twenty thousand dollars already?"

"Oh, you know, a debt here, an Italian suit there . . . One can't be expected to keep track of all their expenditures."

"One most certainly can!" spluttered Dr. Wright. Asha was willing to bet that Dr. Wright was the sort of adult who kept all of his paper receipts to check against his bank statements.

"Carlisle," Dr. Ito said, suddenly businesslike. "Today is Saturday. My lawyer's office opens on Monday at eight a.m. That gives you about forty-one hours before I come after you with my considerable resources. I hope some of that twenty thousand slipped between your couch cushions, because if I were you, I'd be trying to scrounge up enough money for a ticket out of the country."

"But . . . Prudence . . ."

"Forty hours and fifty-nine minutes, Carlisle."

The former artistic director of the Fairfleet Center for the Performing Arts stood up, staring at Dr. Ito with the dull eyes of a man who couldn't quite comprehend his misfortune. He stumbled backward down the porch steps. When he reached solid ground, he turned and ran toward the trees. For all his quick wit, Carlisle was not an especially fast runner. At one point he tripped and fell face-first in the mud by the lake.

Dr. Fairfleet watched Carlisle's flight with amusement. Asha understood. There was nothing better for a lover of games than watching a game take an unexpected turn. Alex understood too. Watching Quentin Carlisle face-plant in the mud was uniquely rewarding.

"Are you really going to let him go?" Dr. Wright asked Dr. Ito, who had remained dispassionate during Carlisle's mad dash for the forest. "That man's a charlatan if ever I met one!"

"Yes, well." Dr. Ito shrugged beneath her shawl. "I have some sympathy for the charlatans of the world. I've sold millions of dollars' worth of paintings I don't even like to a gullible public. In any case, he has just forty hours and fifty-six minutes to get away."

"Good riddance!" Alex said.

"Indeed," Dr. Fairfleet concurred.

There was a prolonged silence at the table. Asha looked at the half-eaten sandwiches, at Carlisle's footprints in the damp earth, at the charter, which lay forgotten by the open puzzle-box. There were no more clues to solve. She felt the same sudden rush of sadness that often hit her at the end of a good book. "So, what now?" she asked. "What do we do now that the mystery's over?"

Dr. Fairfleet gave her a sympathetic smile. "Now we get back to the less exciting but necessary business of life. First, I imagine that some phone calls are in order. Your parents will want to know where you are, and the Waverly

College board of trustees will want to know where *I* am. But don't worry," he added with a reassuring wink, "there will always be other games, other mysteries. In my experience, life doesn't remain unpuzzled for long."

After conducting some of the less exciting but necessary business of life, the detectives and the directors of the Fairfleet Institute, minus one, settled into a lazy afternoon on the lake. Alex and Asha waded in the clear water, minnows dancing around their toes. They kept a keen eye out for blue herons stalking through the reeds.

Eventually, the evening shadows lengthened as the sky turned an inky blue. When it was dark enough, Dr. Fairfleet showed them how to find Sagittarius by looking for the teapot-shaped configuration of stars at its center. Without the light pollution from town, Alex was struck by the sheer number of stars in the sky—uncountable and unaccountable. Asha marveled at the fact that they were searching for the same constellations the Nabataeans would have recognized two thousand years ago and half a world away. Somehow the enormous scale of time and the universe made them feel supremely unimportant and supremely important all at once.

Minnie and Dr. Wright built a bonfire down by the water, while Dr. Fairfleet brought out sparklers that were left over from some summer holiday gone by. The night came alive with scattered light as the fire snapped, the sparklers fizzed gold, and the stars winked overhead.

EPILOGUE

Sunday, September 3rd

On a typical day in the town of Northbrook there were no transitions to celebrate, but on the third of September there were three:

In the first place, September 3rd marked the end of summer vacation for Northbrook public school students. New backpacks had been purchased and stuffed with folders, Post-it Notes, and highlighters. Rumors were swirling about which teachers gave the hardest tests and which eighth graders sold answers to those tests. Asha turned up her nose at these rumors. Alex wondered how much one could make in the answer-selling business.

In the second place, the third of September was Asha's half birthday. Asha and Alex suspected that they were getting too old to celebrate half birthdays, so they decided to observe the occasion as one last tribute to the whims of early childhood before undertaking the very serious business of middle school.

In the third place, and more to the point, September 3rd was exactly fifty days after the conclusion of the Fairfleet affair.

A lot had changed in those fifty days, and a lot hadn't changed at all. Dr. Wright had taken on the responsibilities of the chairman of the Fairfleet Institute. He and Dr. Ito were hiring to fill the vacant directorships at the Museum of Natural History and the Fairfleet Center for the Performing Arts.

Dr. Fairfleet and Minnie were traveling through Europe. Alex and Asha had received three postcards from them so far. Minnie always wrote thoughtful notes, but she never said exactly where they were. The postcards themselves usually featured lesser-known landmarks, leaving the detectives to try to figure out the location, as their mentors intended. So far, they were pretty sure they had postcards from Paris, Madrid, and, of course, Athens. Asha and Alex pinned each postcard to a corkboard in the tree house so that their absent friends felt a little less absent.

They had received one other postcard—a picture of a wide, white beach and clear turquoise water. This postcard featured no friendly note and held no clues to help them figure out where it had come from. It was addressed simply to "Him & Herlock Holmes." Alex pinned this postcard up next to the others. He would never have admitted as much to Asha, but he was delighted to know that Carlisle cared enough to send them cryptic updates. Every detective needs a good nemesis, after all.

As for the A&A Detective Agency, business had never been better. The citizens of Northbrook had been miffed to learn they'd been fooled by Dr. Fairfleet, though they couldn't stay mad at their favorite eccentric millionaire for long. Alex and Asha, on the other hand, were the darlings of the small-town media machine. *The Northbrook Nail* published an article on the front page about the young sleuths, and they were featured on the local news—much to the chagrin of the detectives themselves, who were old enough to know that not all news is cool news. Fortunately, none of their classmates watched the local news, but grandparents with money to burn did. After their segment aired, they started getting all sorts of paying cases.

They helped Mrs. Leicester find her lost schnauzer, Marigold. They determined that Jack Townsend Jr.'s son,

Jack Townsend III, had fled to Chicago in a rage after the controversial reading of Jack Townsend Sr.'s last will and testament. For each of these cases, they received fifty dollars apiece. Asha and Alex also helped moderate a dispute over sandbox rights between the Waters twins who lived down the street. They didn't charge for this last case because it hardly counted as detective work and because Moira and Marvin Waters were only six years old.

Alex and Asha both noticed the irony: as they started getting more and more case requests, they had less and less time to pursue them. Alex worked with Dr. Ito on his digital art projects most afternoons, though he flatly refused to think of himself as an "artistic youth." Asha, meanwhile, was helping Dr. Wright with his review of the cultural artifacts in the Museum of Natural History. Dr. Fairfleet had held up his end of the bargain; the Fairfleet Institute could continue to exhibit the bust of Athena, on loan now from the National Archaeological Museum in Greece. While Minnie was away, Dr. Wright and Asha were receiving help from an exceptionally old man named Egbert, who had come out of retirement to serve as interim archivist for the Institute. Now, with school starting, Alex and Asha would have to be a lot pickier about the cases they decided to take.

On the third of September, the detectives celebrated Asha's half birthday by making her favorite cake: cinnamon spice sponge cake with whipped cream frosting. At first, Alex had been appalled by the lack of chocolate. A cake without a *single* chocolate element seemed downright negligent. But they had made the cake so many times over the years that he had come to associate the flavors with Asha and friendship. He didn't miss the chocolate so much anymore.

After dinner with Asha's parents, they put some leftover cake in a Tupperware container and walked down the street to the tree house. There was a sign taped to the trapdoor that said: NO VISITORS WITHOUT APPOINTMENTS. The sign was just a precaution. It wasn't as though any cigarette-smoking femme fatales ever came up the rope ladder seeking their services. All of their case requests came via email.

In the tree house, Alex stretched out in the hammock while Asha nestled down in one of the beanbag chairs. The lantern in the middle of the floor cast long shadows over the walls—shadows too familiar to be frightening.

It was then that Alex and Asha noticed the box.

It was a large box, about two feet square, wrapped in gold-and-silver paper. The lid, which could be lifted off independently, was topped with the most elaborate gold bow that Asha had ever seen.

As Alex got up to investigate further, the box moved—just a little. There was a thump and a shuffle from within, and the whole gleaming cube slid a couple of inches to the right.

"What is it?" Asha whispered. "And how did it get here?"

"Only one way to find out." Alex approached the box on soft-socked feet and lifted off the lid. They both leaned forward for a better look.

Inside the box was a basset hound puppy, a tiny little thing, each ear as big as the rest of her body. She looked up at Asha and Alex with the saddest, droopiest eyes and let out a heart-wrenching *awoooo*.

"Oh, goodness!" Asha said in a flawless evocation of Minnie Mayflower. She picked up the puppy with both hands, cradling her gently, while Alex opened the note that had been taped to the inside of the lid. This is what the note said:

My dear Asha and Alex,

Please accept this small (but fast-growing) token of my gratitude and affection as you celebrate the end of summer and prepare for your first day of middle school. I have consulted with Mr. and Mrs. Singh, and we agreed that the puppy should live with Asha, but I am counting on both of you to love her and train her and raise her to be a clue-sniffing sidekick worthy of the finest detectives in Northbrook. I look forward to seeing all three of you when Minnie and I return from Europe in October.

Your friend,

Dr. Alistair Fairfleet

Asha had always considered herself a cat person, but her father was allergic, and she saw how a hound could be useful to the agency. She lifted the puppy up so that they were face-to-face and received a little lick on the nose.

"What should we name her?" Alex asked. He already had several ideas, most of which had to do with famous revolutionaries. "How about Karl Barks?"

Asha let her blank face show her disapproval. "She's a girl and a detective agency dog. She should have a good detective name. And no puns, please."

Alex thought for a moment. "Sherlock Bones. Hercule Pawrot."

"What part of *no puns* don't you understand?"

"So, what then? You want to name her something boring like Agatha Christie?"

The puppy stirred in Asha's arms, looked up at Alex, and winked sleepily.

"I think she likes it," Asha said. "We could call her Aggie for short."

The puppy rolled over, revealing a perfect little potbelly for Asha to rub.

"Aggie," Alex said, resigned. It lacked a certain flair, but it seemed to fit, and he had no desire to be an overly controlling puppy parent.

Alex, Asha, and Aggie remained in the tree house until the last of the house lights on Alex's street flickered off. Alex had finished the rest of the cake. Aggie was snoozing on the floor, wrapped up in her own ears. Asha knew that her parents would be expecting her home soon, but she couldn't quite bring herself to leave. She wanted to savor each minute of their last night of freedom.

A soft breeze blew through the branches of the old oak tree, harmonizing with the hum of evening crickets. The tree house smelled like flowers from the garden and cinnamon from the cake and, faintly, of leaves beginning to think of autumn. It was, in short, a very sweet end to a very satisfying summer.

ACKNOWLEDGMENTS

I owe so much to so many people for helping to bring the A&A Detective Agency to the world. Many thanks to my agent, Erin Clyburn, for her input, her acumen, and her tireless effort on behalf of my puzzle mystery; to my editor, Ardi Alspach, for making this book better with each draft and for serving as a gracious guide through the publication process; to Gulnaz Saiyed for her thoughtful feedback; to Júlia Sardà for her beautiful cover art; to everyone at Union Square Kids for their professional dedication and expertise.

To Clare, Connor, Elliot, Eric, and Jessica—I am fortunate to have wonderful friends who are also such talented writers, teachers, and early readers. Endless gratitude to my parents for inspiring my lifelong love of literature and storytelling, and to my brother, Michael, for years of narratives shared and games well played. And to Neil, my first and last reader and my constant counsel—at every turn I have relied on your wisdom and support; a good detective would find your fingerprints all over these pages.

ABOUT THE AUTHOR

K. H. Saxton is an English teacher and boarding school administrator. She lives in Connecticut with her husband and their golden retriever named Goose. After graduating from Yale University, she worked for a year at a school in the United Kingdom before returning to teach in New England. At various stages of her life so far, she has been a violinist, a violist, a pit orchestra musician, an amateur actor, a dabbling dancer, and an assistant theater director; at all stages, she has been an aficionado of the arts. She also loves riddles, crossword puzzles, slow-paced travel, board games, libraries, museums, and good cheese. Many of these things appear in her books.